G000140558

ad bea

MY FAVOURITE
RAILWAY STORIES

In the same series

MY FAVOURITE BALLET STORIES
edited by Beryl Grey

MY FAVOURITE VILLAGE STORIES
edited by Ronald Blythe

MY FAVOURITE MUSIC STORIES
edited by Yehudi Menuhin

MY FAVOURITE MOUNTAINEERING STORIES
edited by John Hunt

MY FAVOURITE ESCAPE STORIES
edited by Pat Reid

and also

MY FAVOURITE STORIES OF LAKELAND
edited by Melvyn Bragg

MY FAVOURITE STORIES OF WALES
edited by Jan Morris

MY FAVOURITE STORIES OF SCOTLAND
edited by John Laurie

MY FAVOURITE STORIES OF IRELAND
edited by Bríd Mahon

and other titles

My Favourite
RAILWAY
STORIES

edited by
PAUL JENNINGS

LUTTERWORTH PRESS
Guildford Surrey England

ISBN 0-7188-2529-2

NOTE
The illustrations are taken from the publishers'
collection, the majority being from their periodical
the *Boy's Own Paper*.

S J 39774

To
NORMAN and PAMMIE HACKFORTH

Set in 12 point Bembo

Printed in Great Britain by
Butler & Tanner Ltd, Frome and London

Contents

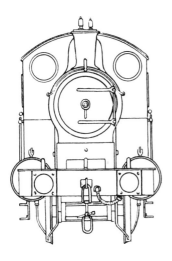

Introduction

Everyone knows the story, occuring in various apocryphal forms, of the man having this nightmare in which he is conducting *Messiah* or playing Hamlet or addressing some huge meeting, or whatever, who then wakes up and finds he *is*.

Is not a person daring to make an anthology called *My Favourite Railway Stories* in such a position? Has he not seen that at every station bookstall (even though there are ever fewer stations and the bookstalls on them tend ever more to close at midday, then at ten, and finally for ever), often next to the pornography section, there are stacks of obviously popular books with titles like *The L.N.W.R. Precursor Family, The Rise of the Midland Railway, Railway Design since 1835, Great British Locomotives . . . ?*

Does such a person, who has never really got quite clear in his mind what the 'lap and lead' component of a valve is (and to be perfectly honest, is not quite sure what back pressure or superheating really are) not fear that the word *railway* in a title will be like that piercing note emitted by the female mosquito to attract the male, like some kind of signal attracting crowds of what are known as Railway Enthusiasts? Will they not gather round him, expecting him to know about everything from the colours of the livery of the old Croydon and Folkestone (or something) to the details of Brunel's S. Devon Atmospheric Railway project?

Well, no. I have met and admired many Railway Enthusiasts, particularly the kind who save all their money, form syndicates, and bring some huge rusting 2-4-2 on a low-loader from that steam graveyard at Barry, South Wales, and spend the next three years of weekends getting it fit to puff majestically up two-thirds of a mile of some siding their preservation society has bought from British Rail. I have had tea with them in their little sheds or in their spanking refurbished stations, from the Dart Valley line to the beautiful Severn Valley (graffito at Bridgnorth station: *Not everyone stops work at 5.30*) and points north. But, technically knowledgeable though they undoubtedly are, they must know in their hearts, like the rest of us, that it is not possible to stop time like this, literally in its tracks.

There is something deeper than simple nostalgia in the great theme of railways—even though, as Kipling remarks in one of the poems which, alas, did not get into this anthology,

'Our King was with us—yesterday!'

(It is the poem of which everyone, especially the crossword compilers, knows the two lines

'Confound Romance! ... And all unseen
Romance brought up the nine-fifteen.')

They were the point at which a clear indication was given to society that industrialization was here to stay.

No doubt this message had reached people in the textile industries in the previous century. Arkwright, Hargreaves, Kay (of the flying shuttle) were men of the eighteenth century; it was in 1767 that the mob is supposed to have attacked Hargreaves's cottage and destroyed his spinning jenny. But it was not until the next century that *everyone* knew that the old rhythms of life were gone for ever. As it progressed, and the remotest country-dweller learnt to guess whether rain was imminent from the apparent nearness of the engine whistle in the wild darkness, we were already half-way to the breakdown of that ancient distinction between urban and rural, between native and traveller, almost simply between old and new, which has finally occurred in our own time of what might be called the Second Horseless Carriage. Now we are all Motoring Man and Television Man.

We are also, thank goodness, Penicillin Man, Painless Dentistry Man. This is an anthology, not an attempt at some huge socio-historical value judgment. There were many Victorians who thought, in their innocence, that steam and the electric telegraph were at last going to bring the human race into one great big happy family. ('So *this* is where it was all leading,' said Henry James sadly when World War I broke out.) Dickens, in the famous *Dombey and Son* passage (page 54), clearly had his doubts. The Duke of Wellington was against railways because he thought they would encourage the working classes to move about too much. In 1865 a man called F. Godwin-Smith, when the GWR were thinking of building workshops in Oxford, wrote to the *Daily News*:

> The moral character of Oxford undergraduates stands at present, I believe, at least as high as that of any band of students in the world ... everybody knows what evils are apt to result when a University is placed in the midst of a great city, and the students are allowed unrestrained access to the population. Everybody knows the character of the students of Paris ....

But surely the main sound that comes down to us from the nineteenth century is the pooming and tantara of innumerable military and civil bands, the huzzas of citizens and the roar of steam as another section of line was ceremonially opened, another station bedecked with tasteful floral displays apostrophising Peace with Prosperity. On the roofline of Ipswich Post Office four allegorical female figures stand against the sky like the saints on top of St Peter's, Rome. They are Industry, Commerce, Steam—and, prophetically, Electricity.

The railways grew at the same time as the vast technical confidence of the nineteenth-century novelist, surveying the entire social scene in a way which somehow made it much more possible also to picture individual souls than it is now, *after* Freud and all that dissection of the psyche and analysis of pleasure (apparently more and more in bedrooms in N.W.1 or Bradford). So there are some pretty giant minds to be found among our writers. But there are also (*pace* the Railway Enthusiasts) evidences of the pioneering thrills and enthusiasms of the first builders, as well as a selection of marginal-comment writing from the days when nobody had to sing, in a very high voice, that this was the Age of the Train. It *was*, then. And, as I hope you will see, not everyone was some kind of oracular prophet about it.

Every anthology has to choose between classics and novelties. Yes, I do Remember Adlestrop, not to mention Skimbleshanks the Railway Cat, and the Whitsun Weddings, even though they aren't here; but I hope I have said enough about the vastness of the theme to excuse their and others' regrettable absence.

I think I know what the real nightmare would be. Having made my choice, and looking over some of the names in it— Tolstoy, Dickens, Chekhov (heavens, what a lot of Russians; that must prove something)—almost a literary *embarras de richesses*, with what opposite doubts would I face the request to compile *My Favourite Motoring Stories?*

Paul Jennings

I

BEGINNINGS

It is only now that we have so many machines for shaping and removing earth that we realise how much amazing physical effort went into the first mighty works. Christian Barman reminds us; and even though John Maclean does not tell us what were the actual verses written, for a characteristically festive line-opening, by the famous Tyneside Poet, Alderman Thos Wilson, we do have T. Baker and the Railway Boom. Hubert Simmons (alias Ernest Struggles) pictures the life (on the Great Western, with such giants as Daniel Gooch, alias Gabriel Gouge, and the well-known signal engineer Spagnoletti, alias Mr Sprigalilly) of the new class of railwaymen; and the Epitaph recalls one death, L.T.C. Rolt's story many deaths, in one of the accidents which, as so often, brought improvements afterwards. William McGonagall supplies one of his inimitable epics, and Charles Grinling recalls the touching willingness, as late as 1892, of people to stay up all night and cheer a new bridge into position.

Opening of the Stockton and Darlington Railway.

Blenkinsop's
Cogs &
Ratchet.

The Pioneers

CHRISTIAN BARMAN

The true type of early railway engineer, the representative for all time of the men who made railways possible, is, of course, George Stephenson himself. The 'inventor and founder of railways' as the *Dictionary of National Biography* simply and grandly calls him, started life by working as a cowherd and was later promoted to the job of picking stones from coal heaps at sixpence a day. At nineteen he painfully practised pothooks; all his life the laboriously acquired arts of reading and writing were so distasteful to him that he never wrote a letter if the writing of it could be avoided, and was hardly able to pick up a book without immediately dropping off to sleep. Yet Emerson said of him (and he said it of no other man) that it was worth while crossing the Atlantic merely to meet him.

The fact is that Stephenson seemed to possess all the qualities of character that really matter. His powerful imagination was steadied and supported by sound and cautious judgment and an indomitable will. How strong that will was we who ride in English trains today can still experience to our cost. The width of our track (and of our trains, which are smaller than those of most countries) was fixed for us by Stephenson. He made up his mind on this point when he was a young man of thirty-four, before the first passenger carriage was built, and he never changed it. It was not old George's habit to change his mind. It happened when he was engaged to build the Stockton and Darlington line. Edward Pease, another great and almost equally obstinate man, ordered him to make the width of his track equal to that of local country carts; with characteristic thoroughness Stephenson had measurements taken of about one hundred carts used by farmers in the neighbourhood. The average width of these carts measured between the wheels at their base was 4 feet $8\frac{1}{2}$ inches. The gauge was good enough for Stephenson for the rest of his life. And having determined his gauge he was prepared to defend it against all comers; he fought and defeated Brunel's bold and forward-looking broad gauge as he later fought and defeated his atmospheric railway. It is true that in the end it was probably Brunel's own obstinacy, not Stephenson's, that gave the victory to Stephenson. The Rennie brothers very reasonably suggested an increase from 4 feet $8\frac{1}{2}$ inches to 5 feet 6 inches. Their proposal was accepted by a number of foreign countries like Spain, Portugal, India and Argentina. It may be that if only Brunel had been willing to accept this compromise our trains today would be roomier and more comfortable than they are or ever can be. Yet, somehow or other, Stephenson always seemed to get the better of his opponents in the end. His staying power knew no discouragement; his path, once chosen, ran as inflexible over every obstacle and every difficulty as the new straight roads of his invention. That is the reason why his handwriting still appears in every corner of our crowded and tortuous English railway map.

In his own day he was known also for another quality which he shares with other engineers of his time: sheer physical toughness. They needed toughness, these men. Lord Wavell has stated that the first essential in a war commander is that he should be robust, that he should be able to withstand the shocks of war. Leadership in the railway age put terrible demands on both body and brain. Already in the eighteenth century engineers had had a foretaste of what was to come. Brindley had taken to his bed when the water was being run into his great canal, and stayed there, paralysed with anxiety, till he knew that all danger was over. During the last stages of the building of Menai suspension bridge, Telford had become ill from lack of sleep. The engineers of the next generation faced more difficult tasks, and even stouter hearts were needed. They worked as men cannot usually work except in times of desperate crisis. In the three years between 1834 and 1837, Stephenson spent a total of roundly thirty months travelling 20,000 miles by post chaise, many of them on night journeys between two full days' work. During the preparatory work on the London and Birmingham line he walked the whole distance between the two cities twenty times. On one occasion he is reported to have dictated letters and memoranda continuously for twelve hours, stopping only when his secretary was on the point of collapse. His vitality was so exuberant that it infected everybody around him. He made ruthless demands on his assistants, but unlike some people of abounding vitality he seems to have had the power of transmitting to them some of his own endurance and patient strength.

Railway building was hard work for all those who took part in it, and this was as true of the men in the drawing office as of those whose duties took them out on the line. John Brunton, who as a young man was responsible for the drawings for an important section of the London to Birmingham line, has left us a picture of the methods of work in Stephenson's office. Two teams of twenty draughtsmen worked continuously in day and night shifts; the whole of the drawings were finished in two weeks, and during that period Brunton himself spent only a single night in bed. A year or two later Vignoles was working under similar pressure to complete the drawings for the Wigan line. 'For three nights,' he wrote in his diary, 'none of us went to bed, and when all was finished every one was completely knocked up. I have, however, accomplished my task; but it has left me full of nervousness and I am reduced to a skeleton'. . . .

It was hard work, but it must have been good fun, too. St George Burke, K.C., who worked closely with Brunel in the promotion of the Great Western Railway Parliamentary bills, has described for us what happened at a time when his offices faced Brunel's on the opposite side of Parliament Street. 'To facilitate our intercourse,' wrote Burke, 'it occurred to Brunel to carry a string across Parliament Street from his chambers to mine, to be connected with a bell, by which he could either call me to the window to receive his telegraphic signals, or, more frequently, to wake me up in the morning when we had occasion to go into the country together, which, it is needless to observe, was of frequent occurrence; and great was the astonishment of the neighbours at this device, the object of which they were unable to comprehend. I believe that at that time he scarcely ever went to bed, though I never remember to have seen him tired or out of spirits. He was a very constant smoker, and would take his nap in an armchair, very frequently with a cigar in his mouth; and if we were to start out of town at five or six o'clock in the morning, it was his frequent practice to rouse me out of bed about three, by means of the bell, when I would invariably find him up and dressed..... No one would have supposed that during the night he had been poring over plans and estimates, and engrossed in serious labours which to most men would have proved destructive of their energies during the following day.'

Led and organised by men like these, armies of powerful labourers supplied the man-power for the building of the lines. These navvies, as they had been called since the canal-building days, were among the most remarkable breeds of people that this country has ever produced. Trevelyan refers to them as 'the nomads of the new world', and adds 'their muscular strength laid its foundation'. Reared from the great rural stock of eighteenth-century England, they were the men and the sons of the men who, dispossessed by the technological revolution in farming, had gone out to build harbours, sea walls, embankments, lighthouses, canals and waterways. Now that the great period of navigation was over, they flocked to the railway works that followed on fast. It was fortunate that such a race of men could be found just at that time. The work to be done was vast and the appliances used by the men and the horses belonged to the world of agriculture rather than to that of engineering. These people of unexampled brawn were watched with astonishment by the other nations of Europe. When English contractors started to build railways in France they brought teams of English navvies with them. The French workmen were horrified at the sight of wheelbarrows carrying three or four hundredweight of earth piled so high that the men behind them could only catch a glimpse of the plank on which they were walking; and at least in one place the army had to be called out to deal with a riot that broke out when the men refused to work with barrows of English design.

Even more difficult and hazardous than work on the open line was the making of tunnels. All the engineers disliked tunnelling. Joseph Locke, who would go to great lengths to avoid their use, gave as the reason for his disapproval the effect of tunnels on the health of railway passengers, but such a reason would hardly be sufficient to justify the construction of some of the most extensive cuttings in the world on his London and Southampton line, where sixteen million cubic feet of earth were moved in cuttings and embankments. Like most railway engineers, he must have remembered the disastrous collapse of the Highgate road tunnel in London in 1812, which made such an impression that it was celebrated in a melodrama entitled *The Highgate Tunnel; or, The Secret Arch.* (The attempt to tunnel through the hill was abandoned and a cutting, the present Archway Road, was undertaken instead.) It must be said that the builders of railways, on the whole, were fortunate in their tunnelling work. There were few accidents as serious as that which occurred when one of the working shafts for the Watford tunnel on the London and Birmingham line fell in and ten men were buried alive. But if the danger to life and limb was less than might have been expected, the difficulties that arose during the progress of the work must at times have seemed almost insuperable.

Water was a terrible enemy. In some places, as on the Midland line in Derbyshire, the navvies worked in diver's dress. In one of the earliest of the tunnels, Kilsby on the London and Birmingham line, water gave so much trouble that anybody except George Stephenson would have given up the job as hopeless. But Stephenson never gave up, though in this instance every other expert was against him. These awe-inspiring works of Kilsby, like the lesser enterprises on the Liverpool and Manchester line, were not required by the natural obstacles along the projected line. They were forced on the builders by the gratuitous opposition of the citizens of Northampton who made Stephenson keep a distance of five miles from the town. Most experts considered Stephenson's plan for a mile and a half of tunnel to be quite impossible. It was unfortunate that a huge bed of wet quicksand, covering several square miles, had somehow been missed during the digging of the trial shafts. Its existence became known only while the work was in progress and the shock of this terrible discovery broke down and killed the contractor. Stephenson, brushing aside all warnings, personally took over the contract, installed steam pumping machines, and pushed on. He narrowly escaped disaster.

'The tunnel, thirty feet high by thirty feet broad, arched at the top as well as the bottom, was formed of bricks laid in cement, and the bricklayers were proceeding in lengths averaging twelve feet when those who were nearest the quicksand, on driving into the roof, were suddenly almost overwhelmed by a deluge of water which burst in upon them. As it was evident that no time was to be lost, a gang of workmen, protected by the extreme power of the engines, were, with their materials, placed on a raft; and while, with the utmost celerity, they were completing the walls of that short length, the water, in spite of every effort to keep it down, rose with such rapidity that, at the conclusion of the work, the men were so near being jammed against the roof that the assistant-engineer, Charles Lean, in charge of the party, jumped overboard, and then, swimming with a rope in his mouth, he towed the raft to the foot of the nearest working shaft, through which he and his men were safely lifted into daylight or, as it is termed by miners, to grass.'

So runs the telling account given by Sir Francis Head. After the flooding the directors of the Company decided to abandon the work, and Stephenson had some difficulty in securing a fortnight's grace. With thirteen steam engines pumping night and day at the rate of 1,800 gallons a minute, with 1,250 men and 200 horses continuously at work, he gradually saw the battle turn in his favour. By the end of the fourteen days the water had begun to fall. The Kilsby tunnel is entered just before the trains to Birmingham reach Rugby. As the traveller passes the bottom of each of the two tall shafts, there is a flash of pale blue daylight and the roar of the wheels is momentarily hushed. It would be fitting if at that moment he were to spare a thought for this dramatic incident in the long battle waged against earth and water by England's greatest engineer.

2
The Railway Boom, 1845

T. BAKER

NEW schemes, not even dream'd of once before,
Were lauded loudly, puff'd off even more
Than e'en the grand trunk-system that imparts
Connection to our chief commercial marts.
Nor was this MANIA, this eccentric roar,
Confin'd alone within Britannia's shore;
It made its way at that eventful time
To every land without respect to clime.
Vast were the schemes that now came forth in France,
Though not so wont in Britain's wake t' advance.
Europe was smitten to the very core,
And thence the MANIA rag'd from shore to shore:
East and West Indies groan'd 'neath the disease,
Its virulence uncheck'd by rolling seas.
Nay, e'en Van Diemen's Land and New South Wales
Determin'd, like the rest, to have their rails.

VAPOR VINCIT OMNIA

3
Newcastle-Carlisle
Opening, 1838

JOHN S. MACLEAN

On this occasion the weather was the very reverse of that experienced on March 9th three years ago. The morning was fair at first, giving promise of a fine day for the large crowds of sightseers and travellers who turned out to take part in the festivities. Heavy rain which fell later in the day soaked many of the unlucky passengers in the open wagons.

The day was celebrated with a ceremonial display almost unequalled in the history of railways. Many flags and banners were carried or floated conspicuously in the air. The memory of 1815 stood out in words 'The Glorious Eighteenth of June', and 'Vapor Vincit Omnia' proclaimed the might of steam. Alderman Thos Wilson of Gateshead, a famous Tyneside poet, celebrated the great occasion in verse★.

At six o'clock in the morning, five trains, drawn respectively by the *Eden*, *Goliath*, *Atlas*, *Samson* and *Hercules*, set off from Carlisle, and at 9.30 the firing of guns announced the arrival of the first train of six carriages at Redheugh containing the Mayor and Corporation and some of the directors from Carlisle who immediately boarded the state barges provided by the Mayor of Newcastle and Trinity

★ At a dinner in 1835 to celebrate the opening of the Blaydon-Hexham section it was announced that a Latin poem of 600 hexameters had been composed in commemoration. The word 'was pronounced *Hexham-eaters* on this occasion'.

House, proceeding to the offices in the Close, and then to the Assembly Rooms to breakfast and to be received by the Mayor of Newcastle. Shortly afterwards the second train arrived from Carlisle drawn by *Goliath*, and in consequence of the rush on to the gangway on Redheugh Quay by the passengers boarding a steam packet, it suddenly collapsed causing over a dozen persons to get a ducking in the river which fortunately was not more than three or four feet deep.

The first train was timed to leave for Carlisle at 11.00 a.m., but on returning to Redheugh about an hour later, the directors and visitors found the carriages occupied. The Gateshead Corporation, by arriving in good time, had secured their seats but the rest of the reserved carriage had been invaded by the crowd.

Matthew Plummer, High Sheriff of Cumberland, the Chairman of the Company, also Sir James Grant and the Mayor of Newcastle, were compelled to look for seats in one of the open carriages on the first train which finally set off about 12.30 p.m. drawn by the *Meteor*. The whole of the locomotive engines belonging to the Company took part in the procession, with the exception of the *Comet*, the *Rapid* acting as pilot running light and carrying the Union Jack in front. The thirteen separate trains were made up of 120 well-filled carriages and wagons holding altogether more than 3,500 passengers. Great enthusiasm was displayed along the route, particularly at Corbridge, Hexham and Haydon Bridge where short stops were made.

Following the *Meteor* with its train of four carriages in which was the Mayor of Newcastle and the Allenheads band, was *Victoria* with nine coaches, *Wellington* with nine, the *Nelson* with seven, the latter two engines ornamented with shields bearing portraits of the heroes of Waterloo and Trafalgar. The *Lightning* with ten coaches contained the Carlisle town band. Then *Tyne* (with its steam organ) drawing nine coaches, and *Carlisle* with eight, *Eden* with ten, and *Goliath* with nineteen wagons holding 600 passengers. Then followed *Atlas* with seventeen vehicles in which travelled the Newcastle and Northumberland Volunteers band. Next was *Samson* with eleven coaches but only a few passengers, and *Newcastle* with nine well-filled coaches carrying a flag inscribed 'Prosperity to Newcastle', and last of all came

Hercules with a train of eight coaches. At Blaydon some time was spent in getting water, and the trains did not leave that station until 1.50 p.m. All the morning a thick fog had covered the banks of the Tyne and now as the procession approached Ryton, the fog changed to rain, which continued to fall all the way to Brampton.

The journey from Blaydon to Carlisle was accomplished in 3 hours 43 minutes, 2 hours 39 minutes being the actual time spent in travelling, an average speed of 23 miles an hour. It was nearly six o'clock when the last train arrived at the Canal Basin at Carlisle, an hour after it was timed to leave. At half-past six a number of passengers arrived at the London Road station where the trains were being marshalled for the return journey. These early comers took possession of the covered carriages, entering by the windows if the doors were locked. So much time was taken in turning the engines and replenishing the tenders with water and coke that it was nearly ten o'clock at night when the return journey began during a thunderstorm. In the open carriages were hundreds of ladies who in expectation of a sunny day and an early return had come in thin light dresses without preparations for wet weather and a night journey. To add to the discomforts of the journey, a short distance from Milton Station, the engine *Carlisle* came into collision with the preceding train; some carriages and a tender were thrown off the line, and two passengers were injured, one having a rib broken and the other a hip dislocated. This accident brought all the trains in the rear to a standstill and there on the verge of the Cumberland fells they were obliged to remain until one o'clock in the morning when the line was cleared. Thousands of people waited all night at Redheugh for news of these trains, the first of which arrived about three o'clock and the last one did not arrive until after 6.00 a.m.

4

AN EPITAPH

ON

OSWALD GARDNER,

Locomotive Engineman,

WHO UNFORTUNATELY LOST HIS LIFE

NEAR THE STOKESFIELD STATION,

NEWCASTLE AND CARLISLE RAILWAY

FROM THE CONNECTING ROD OF

THE ENGINE BREAKING

ON SATURDAY, AUGUST 14th, 1840

HE WAS TWENTY-SEVEN YEARS OF AGE, AND WAS HIGHLY ESTEEMED FOR HIS MANY AMIABLE QUALITIES BY HIS FELLOW-WORKERS. AND HIS DEATH WILL BE LONG LAMENTED BY ALL WHO HAD THE PLEASURE OF HIS ACQUAINTANCE. THESE LINES WERE COMPOSED BY AN UNKNOWN FRIEND AND LEFT AT THE BLAYDON STATION; AND AS A MEMENTO OF THE WORTHINESS OF THE DECEASED, HAVE BEEN PRINTED WITH SOME EMENDATION, AT THE EXPENSE OF HIS FELLOW-WORKMEN.

My *Engine* now is cold and still,
No water does my *boiler* fill;
My *coke* affords its flame no more,
My days of usefulness are o'er;
My *wheels* deny their noted speed;
No more my guiding hand they heed.
My *whistle,* too, has lost its tone,
Its shrill and thrilling sounds are gone.
My *valves* are now thrown open wide.
My *flanges* all refuse to guide.
My *clacks,* also, though once so strong,
Refuse their aid in the busy throng.
No more I feel each urging breath,
My *steam* is now condens'd in death.
Life's *railway's* o'er, each *station's* past.
In death I'm stopp'd and rest at last.
Farewell, dear friends, and cease to weep!
In CHRIST I'm SAFE, in HIM I sleep.

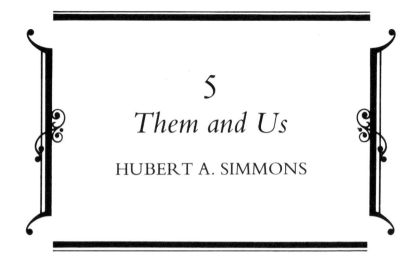

5
Them and Us

HUBERT A. SIMMONS

As the goods clerks were allowed to have a half holiday on
Saturday, with the exception of one clerk who remained to
take the money and invoice out the goods, I had the afternoon at my disposal, and at the invitation of Joe War, I
walked up to see him 'book a few passengers in style,' as he
called it. As I approached the passenger station, I noticed a
large number of cabs plying to and from the station and the
town, and I soon ascertained that the pupils from the college
were the cause of all the extra traffic, and that the vacation
having commenced, they were all hurrying to their homes
by train. The booking office was crammed with them, and
they were pushing one another to get near to the little
pigeon-hole where the tickets were given out. It was with
difficulty that I got to the door of Joe War's office. He did
not take any notice of my knocking, so I called him by name,
and he let me in, hastily re-closing the door and locking it.
Joe was pleased to see me, and he turned up his coat sleeves
as if to perform some conjuring trick.

'Now, my boy,' said he, 'I will show you a move. That's
the British public outside, and I hate them, and this is Joe
War, and I'll let 'em know it. Do you see these boots, old
man,' and so saying, he pulled up his trousers and displayed
some spring-elastic-sided boots, which were getting a little
shabby, 'and do you see these coins,' pointing at two two-
shilling pieces and three shilling coins on the counter. I

looked at the coins, for I never saw any just like them before. 'Ha! ha!' said Joe, 'you don't see the joke! Can't you see that they have had a piece nicked out of them? They are duffers! I should like to wring the neck of that cove up in the cashier's office in London. I'll back he is doing a good thing up there. Every now and then he sends me down a 'duffer', which he swears I took and sent to him. I wouldn't care about that if he didn't nick a piece out of the coin, and then he coolly debits my account with the money. I have to send a good coin in place of it, and then he thinks I am going to see myself robbed like that. What's the odds he is not in with a swim of bad coiners and palms their coins off on us country coves! But I am not quite such a fool. If the British public rob me, I mean robbing them; so I have stuck a bit of lead in the nicks, and they must all go by this very next train. Just count that cash in my till, will you?'

I counted the cash. There was two pounds one shilling and four pence. Joe took out the one shilling and four pence, put in the bad coins, took out good coins to the same value, and by that time the students were clamouring loudly for tickets. The office was quite full of them, and they were thumping the pigeon-hole slide violently.

'Now, Mr British Public,' said Joe, rubbing his hands, 'it wants just seven minutes to the time of train starting, I'll give you gruel!' and so saying he opened the slide for tickets. At least four hands were thrust into the office through the aperture, and twenty voices were heard asking for tickets to different places. Joe decided on one place first, and calling out that all those who wanted tickets for that place would be served first, Joe proceeded to issue the tickets.

The fare was seven shillings and eleven pence. Joe handed the ticket, and receiving in most cases half a sovereign, he promptly put down one penny, called out 'nine shillings', and then adding one shilling change, said 'ten', handing out another and another with a sleight of hand that was marvellous.

He had not calculated it right, as seven shillings eleven pence, one penny and one shilling, only made nine shillings, and each passenger was thus defrauded of one shilling. So I told him of the mistake, but the only reply I got was, 'Shut up, you coon,' so I did not interfere further, and indeed I was afraid they would not all get tickets before the train started.

The bell was then ringing to signal its approach, and two passengers had grabbed their tickets and left their change altogether. I am ashamed to say that I don't think a single passenger by that train received his right change. I made several mental calculations between the tickets and the amounts, but they invariably worked out wrong. The train was detained about three minutes, waiting for the passengers to be booked, but it started at last; and when the whistle sounded, Joe closed the window and danced a hornpipe in the centre of the booking office.

'Ernest,' said he, for he had commenced to call me by my Christian name, 'just look in my cash-drawer and pick me out those "duffer coins".'

I proceeded to hunt amongst huge bowls of silver, but nowhere could I find one.

'Not find one,' said Joe. 'Then where can they be?' and he struck up a song about—

> "Oh where, oh where is my little dog gone,
>   Oh where, oh where is he?
> With his ears cut short and his tail cut long,
>   Oh where, oh where can he be?"

'Ernest,' said Joe, 'just call off the numbers on the bottoms of those tickets that are standing out, and the names of the stations.'

I did this, and with an alacrity that surprised me, Joe put them down in his train book, and called out the total amount wanted for tickets sold by that train.

'Now Master Ernest,' said he, 'count the cash whilst I do a weed,' and Joe seated himself before the office fire and lit a good cigar with all the ease of a prince in his drawing-room.

I counted the silver into pounds, and Joe never troubled even to look at me. In fact he was sitting with his back to me. When I had completed, he enquired the amount. It was two pounds seven shillings in excess of the amount required, not forgetting the two pounds he commenced with. Joe locked the proper amount in the iron safe, kept for the purpose, and adjusting his ticket case pocketed the two pounds seven shillings, closed the cash drawer, and said, 'Come on young man.'

Our first call was at the boot shop, where Joe selected a pair of twenty-one-shilling boots, and I then understood his reason for displaying the old ones to me before booking the train. Next he bought a nice cucumber, and then about four pounds [weight] of salmon, at one shilling per pound.

'There, Master Ernest,' said Joe, 'I must get back to book the up cheap, but you get our landlady to cook this salmon by seven o'clock, and we will have a hot tea for once. Why shouldn't we taste salmon as well as the British public?'

I obeyed Joe's instructions, and at the appointed time the salmon was served up with cucumber and melted butter.

'By jove,' said Joe, 'I forgot the shrimps; but never mind, hand me some of that Cocks' Sauce. That's the first sauce that ever was bottled, my boy, and the old cock that sells it is an old brick★. The other night he went to sleep in the train and came beyond his intended journey. He had his little daughter with him, I think he called her Jessie, and she went to sleep too. The Inspector was going to excess them for coming beyond their journey, but I thought he looked a jolly old chap, so I let him off the excess and took him up to the Lion Hotel. He would make me come and have some wine with him, and then he told me about this sauce. How his father and mother were butler and housekeeper to an old lady, who left them the receipt when she died. The first sauce they made in a stew pan; but the amusing part was how his father advertised it. There were no trains in those days, so he went up the road by wagon to London and took some sauce with him. He used to call at the roadside inns, where the wagoners had their dinners, and pull out a bottle and give them all a drop, and then give what was left to the landlady. Catch a man doing that now. He puts a thundering great advertisement up with a painting of a sick lion in a net, or a likeness of the Queen to catch the eye, and then rides about first class, and does it all by correspondence.'

After supper, I tendered Joe half the cost of the salmon but he would not take it, and we had an argument.

★ Cocks' Sauce was a celebrated product of Reading, first manufactured in 1789.

'Ernest, my boy,' said he, 'that's bunce.'

'Bunce,' said I. 'What's that?'

'You are green,' said Joe. 'Why, bunce is makings. Fancy a chap coming straight from a house agent's office in London and not knowing what bunce is.'

'If you don't mind,' said I, 'I would much rather pay half.'

Joe buttoned his coat, picked his teeth, and crossing his legs, said—

'Now, young man, I know all about you and why you want to pay half, and I must read you just one lesson. There was a time when I was as squeamish as you, and if anybody left a shilling, I called them back, but that time is dead; and if you think you're going to be on a railway and go straight, I tell you, once for all, you will find your mistake out. Why, there is old Peltum, the superintendent, and that Calcraft, the auditor*, if they were to catch you £1 short in your cash, they would have you up before the Board the very next Wednesday, and "sack" is the name for it, straight off. Besides, if a fellow doesn't dress well and keep himself respectable, Peltum would shift him to the goods, and there you can't make a stiver, and must go in rags for the rest of your life. Do you think the Directors imagine for one moment that twenty-two shillings and sixpence per week keeps me? Not they. They know all about it; and when they appoint booking clerks, they ought to say, "There's a place for you; we know you can't live on what we pay you, but go in and do the best you can for yourself; but, by George, don't let us catch you".'

Such was Joe's reasoning, and knowing that he would be offended at any further offer to pay half, I did not proffer it, but I secretly determined to eat no more salmon thus obtained.

'Now then,' said Joe, 'I am going up to the Lion to put just one sov. on a horse that I fancy for the next race. Come along.' Joe having first put on his new boots and his top hat, and provided himself with a silver-mounted cane, cosmetiqued his moustache, and tucked a new silk pocket-handkerchief half into his side coat pocket.

* William Calcraft (1800–79), executioner to the City of London, best-known hangman of his time. Hence the pseudonym.

The waiters all touched their heads, for they had no hats on, to Joe, as he walked into the billiard room of the Lion a recognised swell. There was a bar at one end of it, and a young lady with curls, dressed in black silk, was serving the liquors.

'Allow me, Miss Smart, to introduce my young friend, Mr Struggles, to your notice,' said Joe, and handing to her a bunch of violets which he had bought of a flower girl in the street for twopence, Joe lazily hung over the counter.

Miss Smart half nodded and half bowed to me.

'My young friend has not been about much, Miss Smart,' continued Joe, 'although he has lived in London. Don't you think he is in very good hands?'

'*Very*,' said Miss Smart, with a decided stress on the word.

'By the bye, Miss Smart, has Joe Hobbs, the bookmaker, been in?'

Joe Hobbs had not been in, but he was expected, and he very soon came in and registered Joe's bet at 25 to 1, and the remaining sovereign of the two pounds seven shillings left his pocket for ever.

'Mr War,' said Miss Smart, 'who is that man with the red face playing at billiards? He has been abusing the Railway Company fearfully. Says he went by a train today when the students were going home. That they never opened the window of the booking office until seven minutes before the train started, and that then he was docked one shilling in his change, and had to run for his life to get into the train, and nearly fell between the train and the platform in getting in. He talks of calling on Mr Peltum in the morning to complain.'

'Does he,' said Joe, clenching his teeth. 'I don't know the cad'; and then he muttered to himself, 'All right, Mr British Public; go ahead, but mind how you start.'

The man with the red face was losing his game, and, throwing down his cue, said to his opponent, 'I'm out of form, I got upset this afternoon at the station, and I've not been myself since.'

So saying, he put his coat on, and taking a bamboo-looking walking-stick, was preparing to leave, when he for the first time confronted me.

'If I mistake not,' said he, 'you are the young man who

swindled me out of a shilling in my change at the station today. I hope it may do you good; but I intend to call on Mr Peltum's brother, the Rev. Mr Peltum, in the morning, and if I can get you dismissed, you may rely on my doing my best.'

I assured him that he was mistaken, for although I might have been in the office, I had never booked any one. My assertion was disputed, and I began to feel myself in a very awkward position.

Joe War hastily took off his gold watch and chain, and handing it together with his purse and cane to Miss Smart, he adjusted a large ring on the third finger of his right hand, and strode up to the stranger before I had time to say more.

'Now, Mr Red Face,' said Joe, 'you have made an assertion in a public room before all these gentlemen. If you had a particle of good breeding about you, you would not have done such a thing, but would have written or gone to Peltum. Now I happen to know that this young man,' pointing to me, 'has never booked a passenger in his life, and unless you apologise to him before I count three, you shall have what you deserve.'

'Apologise!' said the man with the red face. 'I swear he was the clerk I saw in the office when I took my ticket.'

'One,' said Joe.

'Pretty thing indeed; first to be robbed, and then to have to apologise to the clerk who robs you.'

'Two,' said Joe.

'If it was a mistake, I suppose it was; but I don't think so.'

'Three,' said Joe, and in a moment he had struck his opponent between the eyes, and he was on his back, and the blood was streaming from a gash in his face close to his eye, caused by Joe's ring. The red-faced stranger got up and made a rush at Joe, but he placed his head in chancery and pummelled his face until he was a mass of blood and bruises. Some of the company separated them, and called out for time. Joe waited for him, and floored him each time with a knock-down blow. The company persuaded him to stop, but Joe declared he would not stop until he apologised. The stranger then rushed for his stick, and unsheathing a long dagger was preparing to rush at Joe. The company suddenly cleared away from him, but a sudden impulse seized me, and with a desperate effort I seized the dagger and wrested it from his grasp. A stout, strong man, about six feet two inches tall, who had been a non-commissioned officer in the Life Guards, then stepped up to me, and requested that I hand him the sword-stick. He re-sheathed it, and, breaking it into two pieces across his knee, thrust it into the fire. At this moment someone who knew the red-faced man came in, and with some persuasion took him away.

Joe retired to the lavatory, had a good wash in cold water, brushed his hair and clothes, reclaimed his watch and purse from Miss Smart, and in five minutes' time was quietly sitting smoking a weed, the admired champion of the room. Miss Smart called him a very naughty man, but she found him a little piece of sticking plaster for one of his knuckles; beyond which he came out of the affray without a scratch.

'Ernest,' said Joe, 'I guess Mr British Public won't turn up to complain to the Rev. Mr Peltum in the morning, neither will he take those black eyes to church.'

The fight and the sword-stick had quite upset me, and I scarcely recollect what reply I made, but I was thankful that matters were no worse, and very glad, indeed, when Joe made up his mind to go home.

6

The Abbots Ripton Disaster

L. T. C. ROLT

On the evening of Friday, January 21st, 1876, a terrific snowstorm accompanied by a north-easterly gale swept across a narrow belt of eastern and middle England. All those who experienced it agreed that they had never seen snow fall so thickly or in such large flakes. Moreover, because the temperature of the ground was much below that of the air, it froze as it fell till telegraph wires became hawsers of ice two inches thick. It was in such conditions of bitter winter darkness and blinding storm that there was played on the Great Northern main line a drama which culminated in the Abbots Ripton disaster.

We must imagine a heavy coal train of thirty-seven wagons rumbling slowly southwards from Peterborough, her driver Joseph Bray and his fireman peering for signals through puckered eyes round the cab side sheets for the spectacle glasses were blinded with snow. Behind them, twenty minutes away, running to time and at full speed, was the up Flying Scotsman. The signalman at Holme had been instructed to shunt the goods to let the Scotsman pass so he had set his signals to danger. To his astonishment he saw the goods run past his box and he immediately reported to his station master that the train was running against signals. The signal boxes south of Holme were Conington, Wood Walton and Abbots Ripton but the first two were not in telegraphic communication with Holme. The Holme signalman therefore telegraphed to Charles Johnson at Abbots Ripton and instructed him to shunt the goods. Meanwhile Joseph Bray was continuing on his way unaware of the fact that the Scotsman was rapidly overhauling him. At Holme the express was sixteen minutes behind him, at Conington thirteen minutes and at Wood Walton nine minutes. Bray and his fireman saw only white 'all clear' lights until they approached Abbots Ripton where they saw a red lamp waved from the box. Expecting to be shunted, they were travelling slowly and were able to pull up at the box. Bray shouted, 'What's up Bobbie?'* and Johnson called down, 'Siding! Shove back, the Scotsman's standing at Wood Walton.' It must have been at this moment that Signalman Rose at Wood Walton saw with dismay the Scotch express fly past his box although all his levers were 'on'. Driver Bray began to back his heavy train into the siding. Six wagons were still on the main line when the express suddenly burst through the curtain of snow and pitched into them in a sidelong collision which flung the locomotive on to its right side with the tender lying across the down main line and the leading coaches piled against it. Like Bray, the enginemen of the Scotsman had seen no danger signals. Fireman Falkinder declared afterwards that he had seen both the Wood Walton signals and the Abbots Ripton distant showing clear white lights. He then put some coal on his fire and looked up to see the obstruction close ahead. He remembered shouting to Driver Catley, 'Whoa! here's some wagons', and then the crash came. Guard Hunt on the goods train was the first to see the approaching express for his van was well down the siding and he described how he saw it pass at full speed with steam on within his train's length of destruction.

The staff at Abbots Ripton made immediate efforts to protect the two blocked lines. The foreman platelayer ran southwards along the down line laying detonators. At 6.45

* Our nickname for a policeman was applied to signalmen.

p.m., only one minute after the collision, Signalman Johnson was trying to get through to Huntingdon signal box to give warning and summon assistance. Repeatedly he signalled 'SP', 'SP', (the code for 'urgent and important') on his telegraph, but received no acknowledgment. After trying for eight minutes he sent the 'obstruction danger' five-beat bell signal to Stukeley cabin, the next block post two and a half miles south. The engine of the goods train was undamaged by the collision and Driver Bray acted with great promptitude and presence of mind. He uncoupled his engine, ordered his fireman to go forward with detonators to protect the down line (not knowing that the platelayer was doing likewise) and sent a relief clerk, Usher, up to the box to obtain permission for him to proceed south. Usher shouted back 'All right for you to go', and Bray set off with his guard, Hunt, on the right of the footplate waving a red lamp.

While these dramatic events were taking place, Driver Will Wilson was speeding northwards through the storm with the 5.30 p.m. express, King's Cross to Leeds, quite unaware of the frantic efforts which were being made to warn him of the danger ahead. He ran into the snow between Tempsford and St Neots. It was blowing strong from the north-east, he said, and he had never known worse conditions in all his time on the footplate. When we recall the apology for a cab which Great Northern express locomotives carried in the 'seventies we may imagine what those conditions must have been like. But Will Wilson was made of stern stuff, and a driver to whom punctuality was a point of honour. 'I was trying all I could to keep time,' he said afterwards. Signalman Johnson had been sending out his desperate and unavailing 'urgent and important' message for four vital minutes when Wilson thundered through Huntingdon at full speed in a flurry of flying snow at 6.49, only four minutes late on schedule. Although neither side realised it at the time, each second counted now in the race between the northbound express and the men of Abbots Ripton who were trying to save it. The next hope was Stukeley, but again Johnson's warning came too late. The train had just swept past Stukeley cabin under clear signals when the bell rang five beats. Hope now centred upon the efforts of the foreman platelayer. He had placed detonators by the Abbots Ripton down distant signal 1,100 yards from the scene of the accident, had run on and was just about to place another when the express bore down upon him running at over fifty miles an hour and he had to step back with the warning detonator still in his hand. It was not until Wilson's engine exploded the detonators at the distant signal that he shut off steam, reversed and whistled for brakes. Immediately afterwards he caught a glimpse of a red lamp waving and heard another engine whistling. This was Hunt and Bray on the goods engine. Guard Hunt had seen the express approaching. He waved his lamp wildly and shouted to Bray 'For God's sake, Joe, blow up, here's a train coming up.' Wilson had been travelling fast on a falling gradient over rails slippery with ice and snow. He could not now pull up in time. To the accompaniment of the flash and fusillade of exploding detonators, the train slid helplessly and was still travelling at from fifteen to twenty miles an hour when Wilson's engine struck the tender of the Scotch express, cut through it and fell over on its near side, the following coaches adding to the pile of wreckage heaped upon both tracks. Fourteen lives

An illustration of the crash from a contemporary magazine

were lost, most of the casualties occuring in this second collision.

It had now become obvious that there was something very wrong with the signals. Signalman Johnson had all his levers 'on' to protect both lines, but Joseph Simpson, the guard of the Leeds express, described how, after the second collision, he walked along the down line towards Peterborough until he met an up express from Manchester and Leeds. It was proceeding slowly, having already been warned by someone whose footprints he saw in the snow ahead of him. When he climbed on to the footplate her driver, whom he knew, drew his attention to the up home signal. 'Joe,' he said, 'look at that signal, what do you call it—showing white or red?' Simpson acknowledged that it was showing clear. It was indeed the case that Bray had been misled and Catley and Falkinder on the Scotsman lured to destruction by false and fatal 'all clear' signals. The Great Northern signals of this date were of the slotted type, in which, when pulled clear, the arm fell into a slot in the signal post. This had become so clogged with snow, driven by the gale and then frozen solid, that the balance weights would not return the arms to danger, the latter not being balanced themselves. To make matters worse, some of the signal wires were covered with three inches of ice. Joshua Pallinder, a signal fitter, told at the enquiry how he had to hack the ice off the Abbots Ripton signals to release the arms from the slotted posts, how he had to tie a 36-pound rail chair to the balance weight of the up distant before it would return. Even when he had freed the arm of the down distant at Wood Walton it automatically dropped back to 'all clear' because of the weight of the frozen snow on the long signal wire.

The conclusions of the Board of Trade inspector, Captain Tyler, are of the greatest interest and had a permanent influence on railway practice. He pointed out how both collisions might have been avoided in spite of the appalling weather conditions. In the first place, in such weather fogmen should have been stationed at signals with detonators, though he appreciated that the storm came on suddenly at a time when the men had just gone to their teas after a hard day's work. But at the same time he censured the station master at Holme for taking no action whatever when his signalman there reported to him that the up goods had run through his signals although he knew that the Scotsman was following. Had he promptly taken proper precautions the express could have been stopped and cautioned at Holme and the first collision averted.

Turning to the second collision he observed that Signalman Johnson at Abbots Ripton might have succeeded in stopping the Leeds express if he had immediately sent the 'obstruction danger' signal to Stukeley instead of first trying, for that vital eight minutes, to get in touch with Huntingdon. But he thought the most culpable of all was the signalman at Huntingdon who, although he denied it, had clearly ignored Johnson's urgent signal and had not, indeed, acknowledged it until 7.05 p.m. He questioned the wisdom of allowing trains to run at such high speeds in such weather conditions and criticised the stopping power of the down express. He also condemned the block system as it was then operated by the Great Northern. He pointed out that even had conditions been perfectly normal there was nothing to prevent the signalman at Abbots Ripton from accepting the Scotch express up to his home signal while the goods train was still shunting only 68 yards ahead. He cited two collisions on the Midland Railway where 'the space interval had been reduced to the thickness of the signal post' and concluded that 'the block system so worked becomes a snare and a delusion'.

At this time it was common practice for all signals to show clear as their normal indication, that is to say they were only raised to danger when required to protect a train. This explains why they became frozen in the clear position. Captain Tyler suggested that in future the opposite should prevail. His recommendation was adopted, and to this day all railway signals show 'danger' and are only cleared to allow a train to pass. The accident had another far-reaching result. The Company rapidly abandoned their slotted post signals and replaced them by the centrally balanced semaphore type falling clear away from the post which became so characteristic a feature of the Great Northern Railway.

This example of the Great Northern Railway was not followed by other companies for many years and it was not until 1892 that balanced signal arms which would automatically fly to danger if disconnected became a positive requirement of the Board of Trade.

7
Saving a Train

WILLIAM McGONAGALL

A poor old woman lived on the line of the Ohio Railway,
Where the train passed near by night and day:
She was a widow, with only one daughter,
Who lived with her in a log-hut
   near a deep gorge of water

Which was spanned o'er from ridge to ridge,
By a strong metal railway bridge;
And she supported herself by raising and selling poultry,
Likewise eggs and berries, in great variety.

She often had to walk to the nearest town,
Which was many miles, but she seldom did frown;
And there she sold her basket of produce right quickly,
Then returned home with her heart full of glee.

The train passed by her hut daily to the town
And the conductor noticed her on the line passing down,
So he gave her a lift, poor soul, many a time,
When he chanced to see her travelling along the line.

The engineman and brakesman to her were very good,
And resolved to help her all they could;
And thought they were not wronging the railway company
By giving the old woman a lift when she felt weary.

And, by thinking so, they were quite right,
For soon an accident occurred in the dead of night,
Which filled the old woman's heart with fright,
When she heard the melted torrents of snow descending
   in the night.

Then the flood arose, and the railway bridge gave way
With a fearful crash and plash,—Oh horror and dismay!
And fell into the seething and yawning gulf below,
Which filled the old woman's heart with woe

Because in another half-hour the train would be due,
So the poor old woman didn't know what to do;
And the rain fell in a flood, and the wind was howling,
And the heavens above seemed angry and scowling.

And alas! there was no telegraph along the line,
And what could she do to warn the train in time,
Because a light wouldn't live a moment in the rain,
But to save the train she resolved
   to strain every vein.

Not a moment was to be lost, so to work she went,
And cut the cords of her bed in a moment;
Then shouldered the side-pieces and head-pieces in all,
Then shouted to her daughter to follow
   as loud as she could bawl.

Then they climbed the steep embankment,
   and there fearlessly stood,
And piled their furniture on the line
   near the roaring flood,
And fired the dry combustibles, which blazed up bright,
Throwing its red light along the line a weird-like sight.

Then the old woman tore her red gown from her back,
And tying it to the end of a stick she wasn't slack;
Then ran up the line, waving it in both hands,
While before with a blazing chair-post,
   her daughter stands.

Then round a curve the red eye of the engine came at last,
Whilst the poor old woman and her daughter stood aghast;
But, thank God, the engine stopped near the roaring fire,
And the train was saved, as the old woman did desire.

And such an old woman is worth her weight in gold,
For saving the train be it told;
She was a heroine, true and bold,
Which should be written on her tombstone in letters of gold.

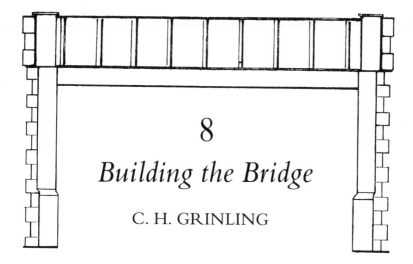

8

Building the Bridge

C. H. GRINLING

Early in June, 1892, the new Maiden Lane tunnel at King's Cross, and at the close of the same month the down single-line tunnel between Southgate and Barnet, were opened for traffic—works which completed the duplicate tracks, both up and down, all the way between King's Cross and Barnet. But by this time two new important improvements had been put in hand within the suburban area. These were the construction of a viaduct over the main lines at Haringey, to form a return road for engines bringing trains to the sidings there—a very difficult work, because it had to be built 'on the skew' with spans of unequal length, and, of course, a sharp rise and fall in gradient—and a further widening at Holloway, to provide a separate track for down goods traffic.

This latter work necessitated the placing of a new large plate-girder bridge across the Holloway Road, and great interest was excited in the locality when the news spread that the crucial part of this work—the moving of the girders into position overhead—was to be carried out as one operation in the small hours of the morning of Sunday, October 2nd, 1892. The two girders, each 110 feet long and ten feet high, were first built up on the south abutment of the bridge on a series of four steel rollers. Then, alongside the abutment, projecting about one foot above its top, two piles were driven some eight feet into the ground. To the bridge itself and to the top of these piles pulley blocks were then fixed,

and to these strong steel wire was attached in connection
with a powerful steam winch placed in a siding some distance
away. On the Thursday, the Stockton Forge Company's
engineers built alongside the southern abutment two large
trestles, each fitted with twelve wheels capable of running
on ordinary rails, and on the Friday morning the bridge was
moved forward by means of the wire and the winch, until
it overhung the abutments by about twenty feet, and slightly
projected over the trestles. Then operations were suspended
until the last tram car should have passed at Saturday mid-
night. Then, despite the hour, a crowd of many thousand
persons collected, and these were with difficulty kept back
by policemen, while the tram rails and pavement were taken
up and replaced by the rails for the trestles which the engineers had ready to hand in sections laid on a strong timber
framework. About 3.30 a.m. these preparations were completed, and then, just as the first streaks of dawn were beginning to light up the faces of the undiminished crowd, the
steam winch was set to work. Motion was at once imparted
to the trestles, and soon the huge mass of the bridge was
moving slowly and steadily forward amid the hearty cheers
of the onlookers. Every now and then a short stoppage had
to be made to ascertain that the tackle had kept in order and
that the strains were equally distributed, but with this exception no hitch occurred, and the girders were got into exact
position and the roadway replaced in time for the passage
underneath it of the first Sunday tram.

II

MAINLINE WRITERS

As the railway brought to an end the long pastoral centuries when nothing moved faster than a horse, it became to writers a rich field of symbol, metaphor and association. For Dickens it was the type of 'universal monster, Death'. In Dostoevsky's The Idiot *(which actually* begins *in a train), Lebedyev is said to have identified 'the star that is called Wormwood' in the Apocalypse, which 'pollutes a third of the world's waters so that many die', with the railways. He answers: 'Not railways, no . . . the railways alone won't pollute the "springs of life", but the whole thing is accursed; the whole tendency of the last few centuries in its general, scientific and materialistic entirety is perhaps really accursed. . . .' Other great writers speak for themselves in this section.*

9

Lust on the Line

EMILE ZOLA

For the association of the railway with lust and murder there is surely nothing to touch Emile Zola's La Bête Humaine, *which presents a picture of life on France's Western Railway which certainly seems to differ a great deal from that of our own dear GWR. One Roubaud, an Assistant Station Manager at Havre, murders Judge Grandmorin after hearing that the old boy had seduced his wife Séverine before he had known her. Then he seems to lose interest in her and she takes up with a real loony, a French Jack the Ripper, an engine driver called Jacques Lantier, who has avoided women until now because he has always been afraid that the moment he saw their white bosoms (Zola was a hundred years ahead of D. H. Lawrence on white bosoms) he would stab them:*

'Did it mean that this was all of such very ancient origin, springing from some evil that womenkind had done to men, born of rancour accumulated in the male through the generations since a first act of deception deep in prehistoric caves? For in these fits he also felt a need to give battle, to master the female, to conquer her, a perverse need to sling her dead body on his back as if an animal killed for food . . .' etc., etc.

But he loves his engine too. Here he is, just after he and Séverine have discovered their mutual love.

In the huge, closed, sooty-black locomotive hangar, lit by tall dusty windows, Jacques' locomotive was among all the others at the head of one of the tracks, ready to leave first. A yard fireman had just re-stoked her and red-hot ashes were falling into the pan below the riddling grate. It was one of those express engines with twin coupled axles, a giant of delicate grace, its huge but light driving wheels with their steel coupling-rods, a broad-bosomed engine, long and powerful in the loin, with all the logic and precision which constitute the sovereign beauty of these metal creatures of precision and power. Like the other engines of the Western Railway Company, in addition to its serial number it bore the name of a station, in this case *Lison*, a place in the Cotentin country. But in his sentimental love for his engine, Jacques had turned Lison into a girl's name. My Lison, he would say, in a fondling, lover's way.

But it was true, he did love his engine with a lover's fondness. He had been driving her for four years now. He had driven others, some easy to handle, some difficult, some full of pluck, some idlers, and he was very clear that every single one had its own character, that many a one was not worth tuppence, just like, as everybody knows, with women of flesh and blood, so that, if he did love this Lison of his, that was because she really had all the qualities of a fine woman. She was gentle, she was responsive to his word, she was easy on the pull-off, and, thanks to a good boiler system, she was a steady puller on the road. It was argued that if she got under way so readily, that was due to the fine quality of her wheel tyres and still more to the fine tuning of her slide-valve gear, just as the fact that she always gave a good head of steam on very little fuel was put down to the quality of the copper of her tubes and the satisfactory layout of her boiler. But Jacques knew that there was something besides that in it, for other engines, identically built, fitted with the same care, failed to exhibit a single one of Lison's qualities. There was a soul, a mystery of engine construction, in it all, a something which the hazards of the hammer add to metal, or the touch of a masterman's hand lends to a vital part: the personality of the engine, its life.

Thus he loved Lison as a grateful male loves a woman, loved her for her quick get-away and quick stopping, for her qualities of a really good mare. He loved her too because in addition to his regular salary she earned him a bonus, being so economical with fuel. She built up her head of steam so well that he was able to save a considerable amount of coal. He had only one thing to reproach her with— she was greedy on lubrication, her cylinders in particular eating up oil at a quite unreasonable rate, she was always hungry for oil, her lust never sated. He made efforts to tune this out of her, but in vain, she got breathless at once. It had to be put down to her temperament. He was now resigned to putting up with this greediness of hers, just as one turns the blind eye to a little failing in people who otherwise are all good qualities, and he was reduced to joining with his fireman in joking about it and saying that, just like any pretty woman, she needed greasing too often.

Earlier in the book Jacques has repulsed the advances of Flora, a level-crossing keeper, from fear he would stab her if he saw her white bosom. Flora gets terribly jealous seeing him and Séverine, radiating joy, sexual fulfilment, etc., on the train to and from Paris week after week. She therefore causes a tremendous accident, by holding back five large horses pulling a huge load of quarry stone (she is virginal but very strong) in front of the express. Fifteen dead, thirty-two seriously injured; but, unfortunately for Flora, Jacques and Séverine are not among them, although Jacques was driving the engine:

At last, Jacques opened his eyes, and without seeming to recognise anybody, dully examined first one, then the other. They meant nothing to him. Then his eyes caught sight of the dying engine, not far away, and into his glance at once came terror, and then an uneasy stare, as his sorrow welled up in him. Yes, Lison was something that he did recognise, and Lison recalled it all, the two blocks of stone barring his road, the terrible impact, the crushing and breaking he had felt simultaneously in her and himself, from which he had recovered but by which she was clearly condemned to die. She was not to blame, she had not got out of control, and if since that little disorder she contracted in the snow she had been less lively, that was not her fault. Besides, one had to for-give inevitable aging, which makes all limbs more sluggish, all joints less flexible. Thus without hesitation he forgave her in his immense grief, seeing her prostrate there in her death throes, growing cold already, her fire fallen out in black cinders, the roar of steam from her shattered loins now but the plaint of a tiny babe. Even so, soiled with earth and spittle as she was, she was still shining and beautiful on her back, prone in that pool of black ash, and her end was the tragic one of a thoroughbred struck down as she galloped by. For a space her ripped-up flanks had revealed the precise movements of her system, the twin heartbeat of her pistons, the blood flow of the steam through her circulating valves and then, like limbs convulsed in pain, her coupling rods had merely shuddered in the great gush of it which had given her life. And in the vast sigh which had emptied her lungs for ever, Lison's spirit had left her body. The immense feminine form sank in its evisceration deeper and deeper into death till at last sweet sleep brought every member peace, and silence, and she was dead. And then the mountain of iron, steel and copper, her mortal remains, the shattered colossus of the frame, the trunk split open, the arms and legs broken away, the inner parts rendered shapeless, all assumed the grim melancholy of an immense human corpse, a world in itself which had known life and from which in pain the living essence had been wrested.

So Flora commits suicide by (how else?) walking into a train in a tunnel. The driver knew it must have been a woman because 'With fragments of skull there were long hairs sticking to the broken head-lamp glass. When they went to search, and found her, they were astonished to find her so white. She was like brilliant marble, her body lying on the up track, where it had been flung by the frightful blow, and the head pulped, but the limbs in their partial nakedness and the wonderful beauty and purity of her athletic form, without a scratch.'

Then Jacques has one of his turns and stabs Séverine, while they are both waiting behind a door to stab Roubaud, but her white bosom, although this obviously isn't the first time he has seen it, is too much for him. However it is Cabuche, a nice but rather thick quarryman, who gets life for this, as does Roubaud, who now confesses to his crime. But the original debauchery of Grandmorin (remember him?) is hushed up, these being the last decadent days of the bourgeois Empire, with the Franco-Prussian War coming up and all. The book ends with Jacques ('since the murder he had known no return of his old trouble, never even gave a thought to such things. The memory of it was obliterated, he was in a state of perfect bodily and mental balance and health') fighting his fireman Pecqueux on the footplate; Pecqueux is angry with Jacques for sleeping with one of his women, called Philomène. They are driving a troop train, which is soon left to its own devices:

Then, with a final effort, Pecqueux flung Jacques out, but, just as Jacques felt space round him, in his desperation he succeeded in clutching at Pecqueux's neck, so convulsively that he dragged his murderer down with him. A double wild cry, voices of murderer and murdered confused in one, broke against the wind and was dispersed into nothingness. They fell together and as these two men, who so long had been like two brothers, went down, the draught of the train drew them in under the wheels, to be cut up, chopped into pieces, still laced together in a terrible embrace. Their bodies were afterwards found headless, legless, two bleeding trunks, with arms still enlaced one about the other, in suffocating grasp.

Devoid of control, the locomotive continued its wild rush through the night. At last this frisky, self-willed young thing, like a young, unbroken mare escaping from her rider, could indulge all the unchecked frenzy of her adolescence and gallop at will across the open land. The boiler was topped with water, the fire-box was roaring wildly, full of coal, and for the next half-hour pressure rose madly and the speed became terrifying. The guard must have fallen asleep, worn out with fatigue, no doubt. And as being herded together body to body like that made the wine go to the soldiers' heads still more, this wild plunge of the train at reckless speed made them crazy with excitement and they yelled their songs at the top of their voices. They swept through Maromme at lightning speed, but their whistle no longer sounded as they came up to signals or rushed through stations. It was the all-out gallop of a maddened wild animal which rushes, head down, blindly at any obstacle. On and on rushed locomotive 608, as if the stridency of her own infuriated breathing made her yet madder still. . . .

By now the telegraph was busy all down the line. Hearts pounded with alarm when men heard the news of this ghost train seen flying through Rouen, through Sotteville, towards

Paris. There was general fear. In front of it ran the regular express, into which this mad thing would crash. Like a wild boar through the forest it swept on its course, regardless of fog signals or red signal lights. At Oisel it all but crashed a shunting engine. Its speed apparently undiminished, it terrified Pont de l'Arche. And again it vanished into the night, rushing on and on, no man knew whither.

What matter the victims which that locomotive might crush in its tracks! Was it not itself plunging on into the future? So why care about blood spilt? Driverless in the darkness, blind, deaf beast let loose among death, on it rushed, packed to the full with cannon-flesh, with soldiers now stupid with fatigue, in drunken song.

10
The Beauties (Part Two)

ANTON CHEKHOV

Another time, after I had become a student, I was travelling by rail to the south. It was May. At one of the stations, I believe it was between Byelgorod and Harkov, I got out of the train to walk about the platform.

The shades of evening were already lying on the station garden, on the platform, and on the fields; the station screened off the sunset, but on the topmost clouds of smoke from the engine, which were tinged with rosy light, one could see the sun had not yet quite vanished.

As I walked up and down the platform I noticed that the greater number of the passengers were standing or walking near a second-class compartment, and that they looked as though some celebrated person were in that compartment. Among the curious whom I met near this compartment I saw, however, an artillery officer who had been my fellow-traveller, an intelligent, cordial, and sympathetic fellow—as people mostly are whom we meet on our travels by chance and with whom we are not long acquainted.

'What are you looking at there?' I asked.

He made no answer, but only indicated with his eyes a feminine figure. It was a young girl of seventeen or eighteen, wearing a Russian dress, with her head bare and a little shawl flung carelessly on one shoulder; not a passenger, but I suppose a sister or daughter of the station master. She was standing near the carriage window, talking to an elderly woman who was in the train. Before I had time to realise what I was seeing, I was suddenly overwhelmed by the feeling I had once experienced in the Armenian village.

The girl was remarkably beautiful, and that was unmistakable to me and to those who were looking at her as I was.

If one is to describe her appearance feature by feature, as the practice is, the only really lovely thing was her thick wavy fair hair, which hung loose with a black ribbon tied round her head; all the other features were either irregular or very ordinary. Either from a peculiar form of coquettishness, or from short-sightedness, her eyes were screwed up, her nose had an undecided tilt, her mouth was small, her profile was feebly and insipidly drawn, her shoulders were narrow and undeveloped for her age—and yet the girl made the impression of being really beautiful, and looking at her, I was able to feel convinced that the Russian face does not need strict regularity in order to be lovely; what is more, that if instead of her turn-up nose the girl had been given a different one, correct and plastically irreproachable like the Armenian girl's, I fancy her face would have lost all its charm from the change.

Standing at the window talking, the girl, shrugging at the evening damp, continually looking round at us, at one moment put her arms akimbo, at the next raised her hands to her head to straighten her hair, talked, laughed, while her face at one moment wore an expression of wonder, the next of horror, and I don't remember a moment when her face and body were at rest. The whole secret and magic of her beauty lay just in these tiny, infinitely elegant movements, in her smile, in the play of her face, in her rapid glances at us, in the combination of the subtle grace of her movements with her youth, her freshness, the purity of her soul that sounded in her laugh and voice, and with the weakness we love so much in children, in birds, in fawns, and in young trees.

It was that butterfly's beauty so in keeping with waltzing, darting about the garden, laughter and gaiety, and incongruous with serious thought, grief, and repose; and it seemed as though a gust of wind blowing over the platform, or a fall of rain, would be enough to wither the fragile body and scatter the capricious beauty like the pollen of a flower.

'So-o! . . .' the officer muttered with a sigh when, after the second bell, we went back to our compartment.

And what that 'So-o' meant I will not undertake to decide.

Perhaps he was sad, and did not want to go away from the beauty and the spring evening into the stuffy train; or perhaps he, like me, was unaccountably sorry for the beauty, for himself, and for me, and for all the passengers, who were listlessly and reluctantly sauntering back to their compartments. As we passed the station window, at which a pale, red-haired telegraphist with upstanding curls and a faded, broad-cheeked face was sitting beside his apparatus, the officer heaved a sigh and said:

'I bet that telegraphist is in love with that pretty girl. To live out in the wilds under one roof with that ethereal creature and not fall in love is beyond the power of man. And what a calamity, my friend! what an ironical fate, to be stooping, unkempt, grey, a decent fellow and not a fool, and to be in love with that pretty, stupid little girl who would never take a scrap of notice of you! Or worse still: imagine that telegraphist is in love, and at the same time married, and that his wife is as stooping, as unkempt, and as decent a person as himself.'

On the platform between our carriage and the next the guard was standing with his elbows on the railing, looking in the direction of the beautiful girl, and his battered, wrinkled, unpleasantly beefy face, exhausted by sleepless nights and the jolting of the train, wore a look of tenderness and of the deepest sadness, as though in that girl he saw happiness, his own youth, soberness, purity, wife, children; as though he were repenting and feeling in his whole being that that girl was not his, and that for him, with his premature old age, his uncouthness, and his beefy face, the ordinary happiness of a man and a passenger was as far away as heaven . . .

The third bell rang, the whistles sounded, and the train slowly moved off. First the guard, the station master, then the garden, the beautiful girl with her exquisitely sly smile, passed before our windows . . .

Putting my head out and looking back, I saw how, looking after the train, she walked along the platform by the window where the telegraph clerk was sitting, smoothed her hair, and ran into the garden. The station no longer screened off the sunset, the plain lay open before us, but the sun had already set and the smoke lay in black clouds over the green, velvety young corn. It was melancholy in the spring air, and in the darkening sky, and in the railway carriage.

The familiar figure of the guard came into the carriage, and he began lighting the candles.

11

Train of Associations

CHARLES DICKENS

In Dombey and Son, *Dickens describes the effect on the suburb of Staggs's Gardens of the coming of the railway.*

There was no such place as Staggs's Gardens. It had vanished from the earth. Where the old rotten summer houses once had stood, palaces now reared their heads, and granite columns of gigantic girth opened a vista to the railway world beyond. The miserable waste ground, where the refuse-matter had been heaped of yore, was swallowed up and gone; and in its frowsy stead were tiers of warehouses, crammed with rich goods and costly merchandise. The old by-streets now swarmed with passengers and vehicles of every kind: the new streets that had stopped disheartened in the mud and wagon-ruts, formed towns within themselves, originating wholesome comforts and conveniences belonging to themselves, and never tried nor thought of until they sprung into existence. Bridges that had led to nothing, led to villas, gardens, churches, healthy public walks. The carcasses of houses, and beginnings of new thoroughfares, had started off upon the line at steam's own speed, and shot away into the country in a monster train.

As to the neighbourhood which had hesitated to acknowledge the railroad in its straggling days, that had grown wise and penitent, as any Christian might in such a case, and now boasted of its powerful and prosperous relation. There were railway patterns in its drapers' shops, and railway journals in the windows of its newsmen. There were railway hotels, coffee-houses, lodging-houses, boarding-houses; railway plans, maps, views, wrappers, bottles, sandwich-boxes, and timetables; railway hackney-coach and cab stands; railway omnibuses, railway streets and buildings, railway hangers-on and parasites, and flatterers out of all calculation. There was even railway time observed in clocks, as if the sun itself had given in.

To and from the heart of this great change, all day and night, throbbing currents rushed and returned incessantly like its life's blood. Crowds of people and mountains of goods, departing and arriving scores upon scores of times in every four-and-twenty hours, produced a fermentation in the place that was always in action. The very houses seemed disposed to pack up and take trips. Wonderful Members of Parliament, who, little more than twenty years before, had made themselves merry with the wild railroad theories of engineers, and given them the liveliest rubs in cross-examination, went down into the north with their watches in their hands, and sent on messages before by the electric telegraph, to say that they were coming. Night and day the conquering engines rumbled at their distant work, or, advancing smoothly to their journey's end, and gliding like tame dragons into the allotted corners grooved out to the inch for their reception, stood bubbling and trembling there, making the walls quake, as if they were dilating with the secret knowledge of great powers yet unsuspected in them, and strong purposes not yet achieved.

But Staggs's Gardens had been cut up root and branch. Oh woe the day when 'not a rood of English ground'—laid out in Staggs's Gardens—is secure!

Later in the story, after the death of his delicate young son Paul, Mr Dombey is travelling by rail to Leamington.

He found no pleasure or relief in the journey. Tortured by these thoughts he carried monotony with him, through the rushing landscape, and hurried headlong, not through a rich and varied country, but a wilderness of blighted plans and gnawing jealousies. The very speed at which the train was whirled along mocked the swift course of the young life that had been borne away so steadily and so inexorably to its fore-doomed end. The power that forced itself upon its iron way—its own—defiant of all paths and roads, piercing through the heart of every obstacle, and dragging living creatures of all classes, ages, and degrees behind it, was a type of the triumphant monster, Death!

Away, with a shriek, and a roar, and a rattle, from the town, burrowing among the dwellings of men and making the streets hum, flashing out into the meadows for a moment, mining in through the damp earth, booming on in darkness and heavy air, bursting out again into the sunny day so bright and wide; away, with a shriek, and a roar, and a rattle, through the fields, through the woods, through the corn, through the hay, through the chalk, through the mould, through the clay, through the rock, among objects close at hand and almost in the grasp, ever flying from the traveller, and a deceitful distance ever moving slowly within him: like as in the track of the remorseless monster, Death!

Through the hollow, on the height, by the heath, by the orchard, by the park, by the garden, over the canal, across the river, where the sheep are feeding, where the mill is going, where the barge is floating, where the dead are lying, where the factory is smoking, where the stream is running, where the village clusters, where the great cathedral rises, where the bleak moor lies, and the wild breeze smoothes or ruffles it at its inconstant will; away, with a shriek, and a roar, and a rattle, and no trace to leave behind but dust and vapour: like as in the track of the remorseless monster, Death!

Breasting the wind and light, the shower and sunshine, away, and still away, it rolls and roars, fierce and rapid, smooth and certain, and great works and massive bridges crossing up above, fall like a beam of shadow an inch broad, upon the eye, and then are lost. Away, and still away, onward and onward ever: glimpses of cottage homes, of houses, mansions, rich estates, of husbandry and handicraft, of people, of old roads and paths that look deserted, small, and insignificant as they are left behind: and so they do, and what else is there but such glimpses, in the track of the indomitable monster, Death!

Away, with a shriek, and a roar, and a rattle, plunging down into the earth again, and working on in such a storm of energy and perseverance, that amidst the darkness and whirlwind the motion seems reversed, and to tend furiously backward, until a ray of light upon the wet wall shows its surface flying past like a fierce stream. Away once more into the day, and through the day, with a shrill yell of exultation, roaring, rattling, tearing on, spurning everything with its dark breath, sometimes pausing for a minute where a crowd of faces are, that in a minute more are not: sometimes lapping water greedily, and before the spout at which it drinks has ceased to drip upon the ground, shrieking, roaring, rattling through the purple distance!

Louder and louder yet, it shrieks and cries as it comes tearing on resistless to the goal: and now its way, still like the way of Death, is strewn with ashes thickly. Everything around is blackened. There are dark pools of water, muddy lanes, and miserable habitations far below. There are jagged walls and falling houses close at hand, and through the battered roofs and broken windows, wretched rooms are seen, where want and fever hide themselves in many wretched shapes, while smoke and crowded gables, and distorted chimneys, and deformity of brick and mortar penning up deformity of mind and body, choke the murky distance. As Mr Dombey looks out of his carriage window, it is never in his thoughts that the monster who has brought him there has let the light of day in on these things: not made or caused them. It was the journey's fitting end, and might have been the end of everything; it was so ruinous and dreary.

So, pursuing the one course of thought, he had the one relentless monster still before him. All things looked black, and cold, and deadly upon him, and he on them. He found a likeness to his misfortune everywhere. There was a remorseless triumph going on about him, and it galled and stung him in his pride and jealousy, whatever form it took: though most of all when it divided with him the love and memory of his lost boy.

12

A Duel

GUY DE MAUPASSANT

The war was over; the Germans were occupying France; the country lay quivering like a beaten wrestler fallen beneath the conqueror's knee.

From frenzied, famished, desperate Paris the first trains went out, going to new frontiers, slowly traversing the countryside and the villages. The first travellers gazed through the windows at the ruined fields and burnt hamlets. At the doors of the houses left standing, Prussian soldiers, wearing their black, brass-spiked helmets, were smoking their pipes, straddling across their chairs. Others were working or talking, as though they were part of the family. When the train went through towns, whole regiments could be seen drilling in the squares, and despite the din of the wheels, the hoarse words of command occasionally reached the travellers' ears.

M. Dubuis, who had been a member of the National Guard of Paris throughout the whole siege, was on his way to Switzerland to join his wife and children, whom he had prudently sent abroad before the invasion.

Hunger and hardships had no whit diminished the rich and peaceable merchant's stout paunch. He had endured the terrible events with miserable resignation and bitter phrases on the cruelty of man. Now that he was nearing the frontier, the war over, he was seeing Prussians for the first time, although he had done his duty on the ramparts and mounted guard on many a cold night.

With angry terror he watched these armed and bearded men installed as though in their own homes on the soil of France, and felt in his heart a sort of fever of impotent patriotism, and with it that deep need and new instinct for prudence which has never left us since.

In his compartment, two Englishmen, come to see things, stared with their calm, inquisitive eyes. They were both stout also, and chatted in their own language, occasionally looking through their guide-book, which they read out loud, trying to recognise the places mentioned in it.

Suddenly the train slowed and stopped at the station of a little town, and a Prussian officer mounted the double step of the carriage with a noisy clattering of his sabre. He was tall, tightly buttoned into his uniform, and bearded to the eyes. His ruddy skin looked as though it were on fire, and his long moustaches, of a paler tone, streamed out on either side of his face, bisecting it.

The English pair promptly began to stare at him with smiles of satisfied curiosity, while M. Dubuis pretended to read a paper. He sat huddled in his corner, like a thief in the presence of a policeman.

The train started again. The Englishmen continued to talk and look for the exact sites of the battles; and suddenly, as one of them was extending his arm towards the horizon in order to point out a village, the Prussian officer remarked in French, stretching out his long legs and lounging forward till he reclined on his back:

'I haf gilled ten Frenchmen in that fillage. I haf took more than von hondred brisoners.'

The Englishmen, deeply interested, at once asked:

'Aoh! What is the name of the village?'

'Pharsbourg,' replied the Prussian, and continued:

'I took those r-rascal Frenchmen by the ears.'

He stared at M. Dubuis, and laughed insolently in his beard.

The train ran on, still passing through occupied hamlets. The German soldiers were to be seen along the roads, at the side of the fields, standing at the corners of fences, or chatting in front of the inns. They covered the earth like locusts.

The officer stretched out his hand:

'If I had been gommander, I vould haf taken Paris, and burnt eferything, and killed eferypody. No more France.'

The Englishmen, out of politeness, replied simply:

'Aoh! yes.'

'In tventy years,' he went on, 'all Europe, all, vill pelong to us. Prussia stronger than all!'

The Englishmen, uneasy, made no reply. Their faces, grown impassive, looked like wax between their long whiskers. Then the Prussian officer began to laugh. And, still reclining on his back, he bragged. He bragged of the crushing of France, he trod down his enemies to the ground; he bragged of the recent conquest of Austria; he bragged about the powerless yet frantic efforts of the provinces to defend themselves, about the transport and the useless artillery. He declared that Bismarck was going to build an iron town out of the captured cannon. And suddenly he thrust his boots against the thigh of M. Dubuis, who turned away his eyes, scarlet to the ears.

The Englishmen appeared to have become uninterested in everything, as though they had found themselves suddenly shut up in their island, far from the noises of the world.

The officer took out his pipe and, gazing fixedly at the Frenchman, asked: 'You haf no tobacco?'

'No, Monsieur,' replied M. Dubuis.

'Blease go and buy some when the drain stops.'

And he burst out laughing again.

'I vill gif you a tip.'

The train whistled and slowed down. It passed the burntout buildings of a station; then stopped altogether.

The German opened the door and took M. Dubuis by the arm:

'Go and do the errand for me, quickly!' he said.

A Prussian detachment occupied the station. Other soldiers stared, standing along the wooden fence. The engine was already whistling for departure. Then, suddenly, M. Dubuis rushed out on to the platform, and, despite the violent gestures of the station master, dashed into the next compartment.

He was alone! He unbuttoned his waistcoat, so violently was his heart beating, and wiped his forehead, panting.

The train stopped again at a station. And suddenly the officer appeared again at the door and got in, soon followed by the two Englishmen, drawn by their curiosity. The German sat down opposite the Frenchman, and, still laughing, said:

'You did not vish to do my errand.'

'No, Monsieur,' replied M. Dubuis.

The train had just started again.

'I vill gut off your moustache to fill my pipe,' said the officer, and thrust out his hand to his neighbour's face.

The Englishmen, still impassive, watched with their steady eyes.

Already the German had grasped a pinch of hair and was tugging at it, when M. Dubuis knocked up his arm with a back-handed blow and, taking him by the neck, flung him back on to his seat. Then, mad with rage, his temples swelling and his eyes bloodshot, still strangling him with one hand, he set to striking him furious blows in the face with his closed fist. The Prussian struggled, trying to draw his sabre or get a grip on his adversary, who was lying on top of him. But M. Dubuis crushed him with the enormous weight of his paunch, and struck and struck without respite, without taking breath, without knowing where the blows were falling. Blood flowed; the throttled German choked, spat out teeth, and strove in vain to fling off the onset of the fat, exasperated man.

The Englishmen had risen and drawn near to get a better view. They stood there, full of pleasure and curiosity, ready to bet on or against either of the combatants.

Suddenly M. Dubuis, exhausted by his monstrous effort, rose and sat back without saying a word.

The Prussian did not fling himself upon him, so bewildered did he remain, dazed with astonishment and pain. When he had recovered his breath, he said:

'If you do not gif me satisfaction vith the pistol, I vill kill you.'

'When you like,' replied M. Dubuis. 'I am entirely at your service.'

'Here is the town of Strasbourg,' said the German: 'I vill take two officers as seconds. I haf time before the train leafs.'

M. Dubuis, who was panting like the engine, asked the Englishmen:

'Will you be my seconds?'

'Aoh! yes!' they both replied simultaneously.

And the train stopped.

In a minute the Prussian had found two comrades, who brought pistols, and they repaired to the ramparts.

The Englishmen kept on pulling out their watches, hurrying the pace, urging on the preliminary preparations, anxious about the time, and fearing to miss their train.

M. Dubuis had never had a pistol in his hands in his life. He was placed twenty paces from his foe.

'Are you ready?' he was asked.

As he answered: 'Yes, Monsieur,' he noticed that one of the Englishmen had put up his umbrella, to keep off the sun.

A voice said: 'Fire!'

M. Dubuis fired, at random, without waiting, and with amazement saw the Prussian standing before him totter, throw up his arms, and fall flat on his nose. He had killed him.

One of the Englishmen uttered an 'Aoh', quivering with pleasure, satisfied curiosity, and happy impatience. The other, still holding his watch in his hand, seized M. Dubuis' arm and led him off, at the double, towards the station.

The first Englishman gave the time as he ran, his fists closed and his elbows tucked into his sides:

'One, two! One, two!'

And all three men trotted on, despite their paunches, like three clowns in a comic paper.

The train was just starting. They jumped into their compartment. Then the Englishmen took off their travelling-caps and waved them in the air, and, three times in succession, they shouted:

'Hip, hip, hip, hurrah!'

Then, one after the other, they gravely offered their right hands to M. Dubuis, and went back and sat down again side by side in their corner.

13
Anna Karenina's Last Journey

LEO TOLSTOY

Sitting on the star-shaped couch waiting for her train, she looked with aversion at the people coming in and out. They were all objectionable to her. She thought of how she would arrive at the station and send him a note, of what she would write, and of how he was at this moment complaining to his mother (not understanding her sufferings) of his position, and of how she would enter the room and what she would say to him. Then she thought of how life might still be happy, and how wretchedly she loved and hated him, and how dreadfully her heart was beating.

The bell rang, and some ugly, insolent young men passed by, hurriedly yet mindful of the impression they were creating. Then Peter, in his livery and gaiters, with his dull, animal face also crossed the room to come and see her into the train. The noisy young men fell silent as she passed them on the platform, and one of them whispered some remark about her to his neighbour—something vile, no doubt. Anna climbed the high step of the railway carriage and sat down in an empty compartment on the once white but now dirty seat. Her bag gave a bounce on the cushion and then was still. With a foolish smile Peter raised his gold-braided hat at the window to take leave of her, and an impudent guard slammed the door and pulled down the catch. A misshapen lady wearing a bustle (Anna mentally undressed the woman and was appalled at her hideousness), followed by a girl laughing affectedly, ran past outside the carriage window.

'Katerina Andreevna has everything, *ma tante!*' cried the little girl.

'Even the girl is grotesque and affected,' thought Anna. To avoid seeing people she got up quickly and seated herself at the opposite window of the empty compartment. A grimy, deformed-looking peasant in a cap from beneath which tufts of his matted hair stuck out, passed by this window, stooping down to the carriage wheels. 'There's something familiar about that deformed peasant,' thought Anna. And remembering her dream she walked over to the opposite door, trembling with fright. The guard opened the door to let in a man and his wife.

'Are you getting out?'

Anna made no reply. Neither the guard nor the passengers getting in noticed, under her veil, the terror on her face. She went back to her corner and sat down. The couple took their seats opposite her and cast stealthy curious glances at her dress. Anna found both husband and wife repellent. The husband asked her if she would object if he smoked, evidently not because he wanted to smoke but in order to get into conversation with her. Receiving her permission, he then began speaking to his wife in French of things he wanted to talk about still less than he wanted to smoke. They made inane remarks to one another, entirely for her benefit. Anna saw clearly that they were bored with one another and hated each other. Nor could such miserable creatures be anything else but hated.

The second bell rang, and was followed by the shifting of luggage, noise, shouting and laughter. It was so clear to Anna that nobody had any cause for joy that this laughter grated on her painfully, and she longed to stop her ears and shut it out. At last the third bell went, the engine whistled and screeched, the coupling chains gave a jerk, and the husband crossed himself.

'It would be interesting to ask him what meaning he attaches to that,' thought Anna, regarding him spitefully. She looked past the lady out of the window at the people standing on the platform who had been seeing the train off and who looked as though they were gliding backwards.

With rhythmic jerks over the joints of the rails, the carriage in which Anna sat rattled past the platform, past a brick wall, past the signals and some other carriages. The wheels slid more smoothly and evenly along the rails, making a slight ringing sound. The bright rays of the evening sun shone through the window, and a little breeze played against the blind. Anna forgot her fellow-passengers. Rocked gently by the motion of the train, she inhaled the fresh air and continued the current of her thoughts.

'Where was it I left off? On the reflection that I couldn't conceive a situation in which life would not be a misery, that we were all created in order to suffer, and that we all know this and all try to invent means for deceiving ourselves. But when you see the truth, what are you to do?'

'Reason has been given to man to enable him to escape from his troubles,' said the lady in French, obviously pleased with her phrase and mouthing it.

The words fitted in with Anna's thoughts.

'To escape from his troubles,' Anna repeated to herself. She glanced at the red-cheeked husband and his thin wife, and saw that the sickly woman considered herself misunderstood, and that the husband was unfaithful to her and encouraged her in that idea of herself. Directing her searchlight upon them, Anna as it were read their history and all the hidden crannies of their souls. But there was nothing of interest, and she resumed her reflections.

'Yes, I am very troubled, and reason was given man that he might escape his troubles. Therefore I must escape. Why not put out the candle when there's nothing more to see, when everything looks obnoxious? But how? Why did that guard run along the footboard? Why do those young men in the next carriage make such a noise? Why do they talk and laugh? Everything is false and evil—all lies and deceit!'

When the train stopped at the station, Anna got out with a crowd of other passengers and shunning them as if they were lepers she stood still on the platform trying to remember why she had come and what it was she had intended doing. Everything that had seemed possible before was now so difficult to grasp, especially in this noisy crowd of ugly people who would not leave her in peace. Porters rushed up offering their services. Young men stamped their heels on the planks of the platform, talking in loud voices and staring at her. The people that tried to get out of her way always dodged to the wrong side. Recollecting that she meant to go on in the train should there be no answer, she stopped a porter and asked him if there was not a coachman anywhere with a note from Count Vronsky.

'Count Vronsky? Someone from there was here just now, to meet Princess Sorokin and her daughter. What is the coachman like?'

As she was talking to the porter, Mihail the coachman, rosy-faced and cheerful, came up in his smart blue coat with a watch-chain, and handed her a note, evidently proud that he had carried out his errand so well. She tore open the note, and her heart contracted even before she had read it.

'Very sorry your note did not catch me. I shall be back at ten,' Vronsky had written in a careless hand.

'Yes, that is what I expected!' she said to herself with a malicious smile.

'All right, you may go home,' she said quietly to Mihail. She spoke softly because the rapid beating of her heart interfered with her breathing. 'No, I won't let you torture me,' she thought, addressing her warning not to him, not to herself, but to the power that made her suffer, and she walked along the platform past the station buildings.

Two servant girls strolling up and down the platform turned their heads to stare at her and made some audible remarks about her dress. 'Real,' they said, referring to the lace she was wearing. The young men would not leave her in peace. They passed by again, peering into her face and talking and laughing in loud, unnatural voices. The station master as he walked by asked her if she was going on in the train. A boy selling kvass never took his eyes off her. 'Oh God, where am I to go?' she thought, continuing farther and farther along the platform. At the end she stopped. Some ladies and children, who had come to meet a gentleman in spectacles and who were laughing and talking noisily, fell silent and scanned her as she drew even with them. She hastened her step and walked away to the edge of the platform. A goods train was approaching. The platform began to shake, and she fancied she was in the train again.

In a flash she remembered the man who had been run

down by the train the day she first met Vronsky, and knew what she had to do. Quickly and lightly she descended the steps that led from the water-tank to the rails, and stopped close to the passing train. She looked at the lower parts of the trucks, at the bolts and chains and the tall iron wheels of the first truck slowly moving up, and tried to measure the point midway between the front and back wheels, and the exact moment when it would be opposite her.

'There,' she said to herself, looking in the shadow of the truck at the mixture of sand and coal dust which covered the sleepers. 'There, in the very middle, and I shall punish him and escape from them all and from myself.'

She wanted to fall half-way between the wheels of the front truck which was drawing level with her. But the red bag which she began to pull from her arm delayed her, and it was too late: the truck had passed. She must wait for the next. A sensation similar to the feeling she always had when bathing, before she took the first plunge, seized her and she crossed herself. The familiar gesture brought back a whole series of memories of when she was a girl, and of her child-hood, and suddenly the darkness that had enveloped every-thing for her lifted, and for an instant life glowed before her with all its past joys. But she did not take her eyes off the wheels of the approaching second truck. And exactly at the moment when the space between the wheels drew level with her she threw aside the red bag and drawing her head down between her shoulders dropped on her hands under the truck, and with a light movement, as though she would rise again at once, sank on to her knees. At that same instance she became horror-struck at what she was doing. 'Where am I? What am I doing? Why?' She tried to get up, to throw herself back; but something huge and relentless struck her on the head and dragged her down on her back. 'God forgive me everything!' she murmured, feeling the impossibility of struggling. A little peasant muttering something was work-ing at the rails. And the candle by which she had been reading the book filled with trouble and deceit, sorrow and evil, flared up with a brighter light, illuminating for her every-thing that before had been enshrouded in darkness, flickered, grew dim and went out for ever.

14

At the Railway Station, Upway

THOMAS HARDY

'There is not much that I can do,
For I've no money that's quite my own!'
   Spoke up the pitying child—
A little boy with a violin
At the station before the train came in,—
   'But I can play my fiddle to you,
And a nice one 'tis, and good in tone!'

The man in the handcuffs smiled;
The constable looked, and he smiled, too,
   As the fiddle began to twang;
And the man in the handcuffs suddenly sang
      With grimful glee:
      'This life so free
       Is the thing for me!'
And the constable smiled, and said no word,
As if unconscious of what he heard;
And so they went on till the train came in—
The convict, and the boy with the violin.

15
Uncovenanted Mercies

RUDYARD KIPLING

If the Order Above be but the reflection of the Order Below, as that Ancient affirms who has had experience of the Orders, it follows that in the Administration of the Universe all Departments must work together.

This explains why Azrael, Angel of Death, and Gabriel, Adam's First Servant and Courier of the Thrones, were talking with the Prince of Darkness in the office of the Archangel of the English, who—Heaven knows—is more English than his people.

Two Guardian Spirits had been reported to the Archangel for allowing their respective charges to meet against Orders. The affair involved Gabriel, as official head of all Guardian Spirits, and also Satan, since Guardian Spirits are ex-human souls, reconditioned for re-issue by the Lower Hierarchy. There was a doubt, too, whether the Orders which the couple had disobeyed were absolute or conditional. And, further, Ruya'il, the female spirit, had refused to tell the Archangel of the English what the woman in her charge had said or thought when she met the man, for whom Kalka'il, the male Guardian Spirit, was responsible. Kalka'il had been equally obstinate; both Spirits sheltering themselves behind the old Ruling:— 'Who knoweth the spirit of man that goeth upward, and the spirit of the beast that goeth downward to the earth?' The Archangel of the English, ever anxious to be just, had therefore invited Azrael, who separates the Spirit from the Flesh, to assist at the inquiry.

The four Powers were going over the case in detail.

'I am afraid,' said Gabriel at last, 'no Guardian Spirit is obliged to—er—give away, as your people say, his or her charge. But'—he turned towards the Angel of Death—'what's your view of the Ruling?'

' "Ecclesiastes, Three, Twenty-one",' Satan prompted.

'Thank you *so* much. I should say that it depends on the interpretation of "Who",' Azrael answered. 'And it is certainly laid down that Whoever Who may be'—his halo paled as he bowed his head—'it is *not* any member of either Hierarchy.'

'So I have always understood,' said Satan.

'To my mind'—the Archangel of the English spoke fretfully—'this lack of—er—loyalty in the rank and file of the G.S. comes from our pernicious system of employing reconditioned souls on such delicate duties.'

The shaft was to Satan's address, who smiled in acknowledgment.

'They have some human weaknesses, of course,' he returned. 'By the way, where on earth were that man and the woman allowed to meet?'

'Under the Clock at ——Terminus, I understand.'

'How interesting! By appointment?'

'Not at all. Ruya'il says that her woman stopped to look for her ticket in her bag. Kalka'il says that his man bumped into her. Pure accident, *but* a breach of Orders—trivial, in my judgment, for—'

'Was it a breach of Orders for Life?' Azrael asked.

He referred to that sentence, written on the frontal sutures of the skull of every three-year-old child, which is supposed, by the less progressive Departments, to foreshadow his or her destiny.

'As a matter of detail,' said the Archangel, 'there *were* Orders for Life—identical in both cases. Here's the copy. But nowadays we rely on training and environment to counteract this sort of auto-suggestion.'

'Let's make sure.' Satan picked up the typed slip, and read aloud:— ' "*If So-and-So shall meet So-and-So, their state at the last shall be such as even Evil itself shall pity.*" H'm! That's not absolutely prohibitive. It's conditional—isn't it? There's great virtue in your "if", and'—he muttered to himself—'it will all come back to me.'

'Nonsense!' the Archangel replied. 'I intend that man and that woman for far better things. Orders for Life nowadays are no more than Oriental flourishes—aren't they?'

But the level-browed Gabriel, in whose Department these trifles lie, was not to be drawn.

'I hope you're right,' said Satan after a pause. 'So you intend that couple for better things?'

Ruya'il, the female Guardian Spirit, a reconditioned human soul like that of the male Kalka'il, is accused with him of having allowed a human couple to meet at a railway station, as they themselves had done in life. Instead of the 'far better things' planned for them by the Archangel of the English, the man dies, after five years in a Rowton House, of an incurable disease. Now the woman is dead too and they in their turn are being reconditioned in Satan's regions . . .

Satan smiled on Hell's own —— Terminus as that would appear to men and women at the end of a hot, stale, sticky, petrol-scented summer afternoon under summer-time—twenty-past six o'clock standing for twenty-past seven.

A train came in. Porters cried the number of its platform; many of the crowd grouped by the barriers, but some stood fast under the Clock, men straightening their ties and women tweaking their hats. An elderly female with a string-bag observed to a stranger: '*I* always think it's best to stay where you promised you would. Less chance o' missing 'im that way.' 'Oh, quite,' the other answered. 'That's what *I* always do'; and then both moved towards the barrier as though drawn by cords.

The passengers filed out—they and the waiting crowd devouring each other with their eyes. Some, misled by a likeness or a half-heard voice, hurried forward crying a name or even stretching out their arms. To cover their error, they would pretend they had made no sign and bury themselves among their uninterested neighbours. As the last passenger came away, a little moan rose from the assembly.

A fat Jew suddenly turned and butted his way back to the ticket collector, who was leaving for another platform.

'Every living soul's out, Sir,' the man began, 'but—thank ye, sir—you can make sure if you like.'

The Jew was already searching beneath each seat and opening each shut door, till, at last, he pulled up in tears at the emptied luggage-van. He was followed on the same errand by a loose-knit person in golfing-kit, seeking, he said, a bag of clubs, who swore bitterly when a featureless woman behind him asked: '*Was* you looking for a sweetheart, ducky?'

Another train was called. The crowd moved over—some hopeful in step and bearing; others upheld only by desperate will. Several ostentatiously absorbed themselves in newspapers and magazines round the bookstalls; but their attention would not hold and when people brushed against them they jumped.

'They are all under moderately high tension,' Satan said. 'Come into the Hotel—it's less public there—in case any of them come unstuck.'

The Archangels moved slowly till they were blocked by a seedy-looking person button-holing the Station Master between two barrows of unlabelled luggage. He talked thickly. The official disengaged himself with practised skill. 'That's all right, Sir. *I* understand,' he said. 'Now, if I was you I'd slip over to the Hotel and sit down and wait a bit. You can be quite sure, Sir, that the instant your friend arrives I'll slip over and advise you.'

The man, muttering and staring, drifted on.

'That's him,' said Satan. '"And behold he *was* in My hand"—with a vengeance. Did you hear him giving his titles to impress the Station Master?'

'What will happen to him?' said Gabriel.

'One can't be certain. My Departmental Heads are independent in their own spheres. They arrange all sorts of effects. There's one, yonder, for instance, that 'ud never be allowed in the other station up above.'

A woman with a concertina and a tin cup took her stand on the kerb of the road by Number One platform, where a crowd was awaiting a train. After a pitiful flourish she began to sing:—

'The Sun stands still in Heaven—
　Dusk and the stars delay.
There is no order given
　To cut the throat of the day.
My Glory is gone with my Power,
　Only my torments remain.
Hear me! Oh, hear me!
All things wait on the hour
　That sets me my doom again.'

But the song seemed unpopular, and few coins fell into the cup.

'They used to pay anything you please to hear her—once,' Satan said, and gave her name. 'She's saving up her pennies now to escape.'

'Do they ever?' Gabriel asked.

'Oh, yes—often. They get clear away till—the very last. Then they're brought back again. It's an old Inquisition effect, but they never fail to react to it. You'll see them in the Reading-Rooms making their plans and looking up Continental Bradshaws. By the way, we've taken some liberties with the decorations of the Hotel itself. I hope you'll approve.'

He ushered them into an enormously enlarged Terminus Hotel with passages and suites of public rooms, giving on to a further confusion of corridors and saloons. Through this maze men and women wandered and whispered, opening doors into hushed halls whence polite attendants reconducted them to continue their cycle of hopeless search elsewhere. Others, at little writing tables in the suites of over-heated rooms, made notes for honeymoons, as Satan had said, from the Bradshaws and steamer-folders, or wrote long letters which they posted furtively. Often, one of them would hurry out into the yard, with some idea of stopping a taxi which seemed to be carrying away a known face. And there were women who fished frayed correspondence out of their vanity-bags and read it with moist eyes close up to the windows.

'Everything is provided for—"according to their own imaginations",' said Satan with some pride. 'Now I wonder what sort of test our man will—'

The seedy-looking person was writing busily when a page handed him a telegram. He turned, his face transfigured with joy, read, stared deeply at the messenger, and collapsed in a fit.

Satan picked up the paper which ran:— *'Reconsidered. Forgive. Forget.'*

'Tck!' said Satan. 'That isn't quite cricket. But we'll see how he takes it.'

Well-trained attendants bore the snorting, inert body out, into a little side-room, and laid it on a couch. When Satan and the others entered they found a competent-looking doctor in charge.

'"He that sinneth—let him fall into the hands of the Physician",' said Satan. 'I wonder what choice he'll make?'

'Has he any?' said Gabriel.

'Always. This is his last test. I can't say I exactly approve of the means, but if one interferes with one's subordinates it weakens initiative.'

'Do you mean to say, then, that that telegram was forged?' cried Gabriel hotly.

'"There are lying spirits also",' was the smooth answer. 'Wait and see.'

The man had been brought to with brandy and sal volatile. As he recovered consciousness he groaned.

'I remember now,' said he.

'You needn't;' the doctor spoke slowly. 'We can take away your memory—'

'If—if,' said Satan, as one prompting a discourteous child.

'If you please,' the doctor went on, looking Satan full in the face, and adding under his breath:— 'Am I in charge here or are You? "Who knoweth—"'

'If I please?' the man stammered.

'Yes. If you authorise me,' the doctor went on.

'Then what becomes of *me*?'

'You'll be free from that pain at any rate. Do you authorise me?'

'I do not. I'll see you damned first.'

The doctor's face lit, but his answer was not cheering.

'Then you'd better go.'

'Go? Where in Hell to?'

'That's not my business. This room's needed for other patients.'

'Well, if that's the case, I suppose I'd better.' He rebuttoned his loosed flannel shirt all awry, rolled off the couch, and fumbled towards the door, where he turned and said thickly:— 'Look here—I've got something to say—I think ... I—I charge you at the Judgment—make it plain. Make it plain, y'know ... I charge you—'

But whatever the charge may have been, it ended in indistinct mutterings as he went out, and the doctor followed him with the bottle of spirits that had clogged his tongue.

'There!' said Satan. 'You've seen a full test for Ultimate Breaking Strain.'

'But now?' Gabriel demanded.

'Why do you ask?'

'Because it was written: "*Even Evil itself shall pity*".'

'I told you long ago it would all be laid on me at last,' said Satan bitterly.

Here Azrael interposed, icy and resplendent. 'My orders,' said he, 'are to dismiss to the Mercy. Where is it?'

Satan put out his hand, but did not speak.

The three waited in that casualty room, with its porcelain washstand beneath the glass shelf of bottles, its oxygen cylinders tucked under the leatherette couch, and its heart-lowering smell of spent anaesthetics—waited till the agony of waiting that shuffled and mumbled outside crept in and laid hold; dimming, first, the lustre of their pinions; bowing, next, their shoulders as the motes in the never-shifted sunbeam filtered through it and settled on them, masking, finally, the radiance of Robe, Sword, and Very Halo, till only their eyes had light.

The long groan broke first from Azrael's lips. 'How long?' he muttered. 'How long?' But Satan sat dumb and hooded under cover of his wings.

There was a flurry of hysterics at the opening door. An uniformed nurse half supported, half led a woman to the couch.

'But I can't! I mustn't!' the woman protested, striving to push away the hands. 'I—I've got an appointment. I've got to meet the 7.12. I have really. It's rather—you don't *know* how important it is. Won't you let me go? *Please*, let me go! If you'll let me go, I'll give you all my diamonds.'

'Just a little lay-down and a nice cup o' tea. I'll fetch it in a minute,' the nurse cooed.

'Tea? How do I know it won't be poisoned. It *will* be poisoned—I know it will. Let me go! I'll tell the police if you don't let me go! I'll tell—I'll tell! Oh God!—who can I tell? ... Dick! Dick! They're trying to drug me! Come and help me! Oh, help me! It's *me*, Dickie!'

Presently the unbridled screams exhausted themselves and turned into choking, confidential, sobbing whispers: 'Nursie! I'm *so* sorry I made an exhibition of myself just now. I won't do it again—on my honour I won't—if you'll just let me—just let me slip out to meet the 7.12. I'll be back the minute it's in, and then I'll be good. *Please*, take your arm away!'

But it was round her already. The nurse's head bent down as she blew softly on the woman's forehead till the grey hair parted and the Three could see the Order for Life, where it had been first written. The body began to relax for sleep.

'Don't—don't be so silly,' she murmured. 'Well, only for a minute, then. You mustn't make me late for the 7.12, because—because ... Oh! Don't forget ... "I charge you at the Judgment make it plain—I charge you—"' She ceased. The nurse looked as Kalka'il had done, straight into Satan's eyes, and:— 'Go!' she commanded.

Satan bowed his head.

There was a knock, a scrabbling at the door, and the seedy-looking man shambled in.

'Sorry!' he began, 'but I think I left my hat here.'

The woman on the couch waked and turning, chin in hand, chuckled deliciously:— 'What *does* it matter now, dear?'

The Three found themselves whirled into the Void—two of them a little ruffled, the third somewhat apologetic.

'How did it happen?' Gabriel smoothed his plumes.

'Well—as a matter of fact, we were rather ordered away,' said Satan.

'Ordered away? *I*?' Azrael cried.

'Not to mention your senior in the Service,' Satan answered. 'I don't know whether you noticed that that nurse happened to be Ruya'il—'

'Then I shall take official action.' But Azrael's face belied his speech.

'I think you'll find she is protected by that ruling you have so lucidly explained to our young friend. It *all* turns upon the interpretation of "Who," you know.'

'Even so,' said Gabriel, 'that does not excuse the neck-and-crop abruptness—the cinema-like trick—of our—our expulsion.'

'I'm afraid, as the little girl said about her spitting at her nurse, that that was *my* invention. But, my Brothers'—the Prince of Darkness smiled—'did you *really* think that we were needed there much longer?'

III

PURE FICTION

Victor L. Whitechurch may have written on other themes, but all his stories in the Strand Magazine *seem to involve trains. It was a hard decision to exclude* Special Working Instructions, *in which a humble country station master foils a bomb attack on the Tsar of Russia, no less; but the story reprinted here must surely occupy the top, indeed the only place in this section, if only for the marvellous dialogue:*

> *'Curse you, let go!' he cried.*
> *'Not I,' I shouted back.*
> *'Then take that,' he replied. . . .*

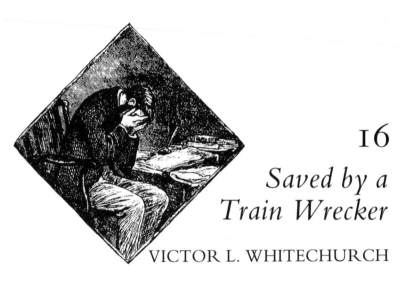

16
Saved by a Train Wrecker

VICTOR L. WHITECHURCH

'I think you had better attempt no explanation, Mr Halbon,' the senior partner was saying to me, very quietly. 'No,' he went on, as I was on the point of interrupting him, 'either to excuse or to incriminate yourself. For the sake of your father, who was one of the staunchest and best servants the firm ever possessed, and for the sake of his widow, Mr Sampson and myself have determined to make his son every allowance. As the matter stands there is a balance of ninety-seven pounds unaccounted for, and you are the only person who can make it right. If the amount is—ahem!—replaced by this day fortnight, nothing more will be said. But if not—'

'Then,' went on Mr Sampson, the junior partner, 'the firm will require your services no longer, Mr Halbon. Possibly, for the sake of those whom Mr Marsh mentioned, we shall not take any more stringent measures; but, of course, such a dismissal, without reason or references, would be the ruin of you. We trust, therefore, that you will be able to rectify the mistake. Good afternoon.'

Ruin! That was just the word for it all, and it rang in my ears with terrible significance as I left the presence of the two partners and took my seat at a desk in the office outside. For although they had not named the word, the terrible charge that was staring me in the face was embezzlement. They had discovered it all. Fool that I had been; alas, the duplicate of many. Not half-a-dozen years out of my teens, with a berth that many an older man might have envied, the under-cashier in the wealthy firm of Marsh and Sampson, of Silk-minster, one of the largest houses in the Midlands, a business in which my father had seen fifty years' service, with a good and increasing salary, and a certain prospect of advancement and retiring pension, that was the position from which I, Frank Halbon, had now every chance of falling. It was the old story—tipsters' advertisements, turfy associates, a bulky betting book, bad starters and worse losers, debts of honour, and threatened exposure, and with it all the constant handling of cash. And so the temptation came. Like many another, I simply 'borrowed it'—nothing more. But before I had time to pay it back the hideous transaction stood revealed, and I knew that my employers regarded me as a thief. And yet they were giving me one chance: just one chance for hon-our—for everything that makes life worth living—a breath-ing spell of a fortnight.

Could I do it? I asked myself the question that night in the solitude of my lodgings. I had been invited out to spend the evening at the house of my *fiancée*. Alas, I dared not face her now. So I sat alone in my agony of anxious thought. Time after time I counted out my resources. The utmost I could scrape together was twenty-four shillings, and, look where I would, I could not see my way to laying my hand on more.

The game was up; that was evident. And out of the situation there grew the desire, stronger and stronger, to get away, anywhere from Silkminster—to London, whither every fortune-hunter or fortune-loser turns his steps. At length a definite plan took possession of me. I had one article of value left, my bicycle, and I determined to ride it up to London, a distance of a hundred odd miles or so, and sell it when I got there. More than that, I made up my mind to start that very night. I was just in the mood for it. I wanted to do something, and here was the chance.

Hastily I packed a few things in my bicycle 'hold-all', filled my lamp, knocked at my landlady's door, and said:

'I am going for a long ride, Mrs Smith—to see a friend. He'll be almost sure to ask me to stay the night, so don't expect me till tomorrow evening.'

'Lor', sir,' said Mrs Smith, 'you're going rather sudden, ain't you?'

I had been with her for some years, and she was quite devoted to me. I felt the parting—the first wrench from the world of my friends.

'Yes,' I said, hastily, 'I have made up my mind rather quickly. Good night, Mrs Smith.'

And in another minute I was bowling through the suburbs of Silkminster, until the houses became more and more scattered, the lamp-posts began to disappear, and at length I was out in the open country speeding away on the road that led to London.

It must have been after half-past eight when I started. It was a dark night, but I knew this part of the road pretty well, and was putting in a good ten miles an hour. Just before eleven o'clock I pulled up for a few minutes in the little town of Dullminster, and refreshed myself with a pint of ale at an inn.

'Don't ye want a bed for the night?' asked the landlord, seeing my dusty condition.

'Oh, I think I'll get on a bit farther,' I replied.

'A bit farther? Which way are ye ridin', young man?'

'Towards London.'

'Lunnon, eh? Well, there ain't a decent place till ye get to Egghurst, and that's a good fourteen miles further, through a lonesome bit o' country, too. And it's a chance but what ye'll get none there so late. Better stop, sir!'

But he urged me in vain. Foolish as I knew it was to go on, the demon of unrest held unbounded possession of me, and I determined to ride till I could go no farther—it was the only thing that took me at all out of myself. So, once more mounting my machine, I was soon pedalling along through the lonely darkness.

Dullminster was now a good five miles behind me, and I had entered upon a stretch of road that was more than usually dreary and secluded. On my right was an open expanse of common, and on my left, on the top of an embankment, the main line of the Great West-Northern Railway ran for some two or three miles parallel with the road, a hedge between me and the bottom of the embankment. The momentary flash of a warning red light on a signal-post as I began riding

by the side of this embankment set my mind flowing in a
new channel. The whole country had recently been aroused
to the sense of a terrible danger. The most cold-blooded and
dastardly attempts were being made on certain of our great
trunk railways to wreck express trains. Some of these attempts were successful, and more than one accident was the
result; some were discovered only just in time to prevent an
appalling disaster; while others fortunately proved powerless
to upset the magnificent engines and trains for which they
were intended.

In spite of every precaution, in spite of systems of patrol-
ling the line and the work of scores of detectives, the mis-
creant or miscreants who plied this abominable trade remained undetected.

Engine drivers, one of the pluckiest class of men in the
kingdom, grew nervous and distrustful. The footplate became a post that meant a terrible and sudden danger. Strong
men clutched tremblingly at the regulator handle as they
dashed away through the open country in the darkness of
the night, and heaved a sigh of relief as they signed 'off duty'
at the journey's end. Many a man actually refused promotion
point-blank because he feared to drive a night express. The
matter was, in short, becoming serious, and more than one
railway company offered a very large reward for the discovery and arrest of the train-wrecking fiend. All this flashed
across me as I plodded along, slowly now, for I was riding
on rising ground, and my legs were beginning to give out a
bit. I had ridden over thirty miles with only a few minutes'
stop, and the nervous and physical strain was telling on me
a little.

Suddenly, as I was riding thus slowly, I happened to glance
upward at the railway embankment, and started violently at
what I saw. There, outlined against the dim sky, was the
figure of a man, now standing, now stooping downward,
seemingly doing something to the metals. The situation
flashed across me in a moment. It was the train-wrecking fiend
at work! Carefully I alighted from my machine, making up
my mind the while how to act. The whole thing came as a
flood of relief to me. If he were really placing something on
the line he was a desperate fellow, and to attack him would
be desperate—just the very thing for a man in my mood.

And then there came across me another thought. The Great West-Northern had offered a hundred pounds reward. What if I should win it? If so, I was saved!

This idea gave me courage as I clambered over the low hedge and crawled stealthily up the embankment. At length my head came on a level with the top. Good! He had seen and heard nothing. There he was stooping down with his back towards me, lashing something with a rope to the down metals. Ten yards separated us. Setting my teeth, I prepared for the attack.

With a spring I was upon him; but too late. He had heard me as soon as I left the grassy slope and my feet sounded upon the ballast, and in a moment he was on his legs and facing me.

I managed to get in one good blow under his guard with my left hand, which caught him square on the jaw, and with my right hand I seized him by the collar.

'Curse you, let go!' he cried.

'Not I,' I shouted back.

'Then take that,' he replied.

Dashing through the darkness of the night—

There was a glitter of steel as he raised his right hand aloft and struck at my breast. But I was too quick for him. Half turning the blow aside, I caught it on the left forearm. I felt the knife slip up under my sleeve, and the sharp point as it entered my flesh. That only gave me redoubled fury. Releasing my grip on his collar, I gave his right elbow an upward blow, that sent the knife spinning away out of his hand right down the embankment, and the next instant I had dodged to the left, made a feint of rushing past him, and had tripped him up with a heavy back-throw with my right arm and leg—a dodge which I had picked up during a holiday in Cornwall. He fell, with an oath, striking the back of his head against the rail, and lay there, stunned, like a log. The battle was mine!

But there was more to be done and no time to be lost. I had to remove the obstructions from the metals and to secure my prisoner. I wanted light on the scene. Hastily I dashed down the embankment, took off my bicycle lamp, and hurried back again. Then I saw the extent of his devilment.

He had managed to get three old sleepers, which were probably lying by the side of the track awaiting removal. Two of these he had lashed firmly across the metals, with a space of about a couple of feet between. The third he had been in the act of securing between them, pointing at an angle towards the train, so that it would catch under the bed-plate of the engine and wreck the works.

The third sleeper I removed. Then I took the piece of rope he had been about to use, and tied the wretch's arms behind him, lashing his feet together also. Having disposed of him, I was turning my attention to the other two sleepers, when an ominous roar in the distance, in the direction of London, startled me. A train was coming! With a yell of despair, I set to work at those ropes. It was no use. I could not undo them in time. I felt in my pockets—no! I had left my knife at home. Ah, there was the train-wrecker's weapon! Where was it? Alas! it would have taken me too much time to find it in the long grass of the embankment. With horror, I glanced ahead. There, in the distance, were two gleaming lights of the approaching train. How could I stop it?

As I asked myself this question I felt something warm trickling from my left arm. I turned my lantern on it.

Blood—dripping red blood from the knife-wound, which I had forgotten.

Ah! An inspiration. And with a prayer that it might not be too late, I proceeded to put it into execution. Drawing out my handkerchief I quickly applied it to my arm. In three or four seconds it was saturated with blood.

I glanced ahead again. Oh, those lights! They were only about half a mile from me now.

Hastily I folded the dripping handkerchief twice or thrice, and stretched it across the face of my bicycle lamp.

Eureka! I held in my hand a red light!

Stumbling, running, leaping, I rushed towards the train, waving my extemporised danger-signal frantically as I did so. The headlights gleamed brighter and brighter, the roar became nearer and nearer. Would they never stop? Ah! A whistle. A shriek in the night as of a startled wild animal. And then a rasping and a grating of brake-blocks, a stream of flying sparks from the rails as the wheels dragged along them, a glare of light in my very face, and a hoarse voice from the footplate.

'What's up, then? D'ye know you're stopping the Silkminster Express?'

'Thank God, I have!' I answered. And then for a few minutes all was black—the excitement and the loss of blood were too much for me. When I came to there was a crowd of passengers around me, and they gave me some stimulant.

'Have they got him?' I asked.

'Got him? Aye, we've got him,' said the guard, 'and we won't let him go in a hurry. You tied him up pretty tight. Lucky you stopped us, for we'd have been wrecked certain. But it's the rummiest danger-signal I ever heard of. Now then,' he added, 'take your seats, please. The line's clear now. What can we do with you, sir?'

'I'll go with you to Silkminster,' I said. 'I live there. And I think you'll carry my bicycle without charging for it, eh?'

They got my machine from the road, and I travelled in a first-class carriage back to Silkminster. The kindly guard, who had a knowledge of ambulance work, had bound up my wound, which was a very slight one. One of my travelling companions, curiously enough, was a director of the line, and to him I told the story how I had captured the train-wrecker. He congratulated me heartily, and told me that the company would certainly pay me the reward.

'Excuse me,' I said, 'but may I ask for it at once—that is, within this fortnight? The truth is that the money is a god-send to me. It will save me from ruin.'

And it did. A week afterwards I was able to walk into the partners' office with my books properly balanced. Mr Marsh shook me by the hand.

'We will not ask,' he said, 'for any explanation of the mistake or how it has been rectified. We only trust that our method of dealing with you will prevent such a mistake from ever occuring again, for in that case not even such a plucky action as that which you achieved last week—or the result of it—will save you. But now we trust the matter is at an end for ever.'

And so it was. I do not think the partners will have cause to complain of me again. And the day that I saw Joseph Berch, ex-servant of the Great West-Northern, discharged in disgrace, sentenced to seven years' penal servitude for attempting to wreck the express, I could not help inwardly thanking the wretch for saving me from ruin and giving me back all.

IV

HALF FARES

Pretty strict rules get laid down about Writing For Children these days. Protagonists must be children that readers can 'identify with' (so what about all those princes,youngest sons of millers, etc.?), classless (i.e. not middle-class, so where does that put E. Nesbit?), easy on fantasy and magic (L. Carroll, move over) ... and you couldn't call Saki a Children's Writer. Never mind; there will always be a connection between railways, proper steam railways, and children. What a pity this book hasn't got a sound track, otherwise BBC TV's enchanting Ivor the Engine *would certainly be in too.*

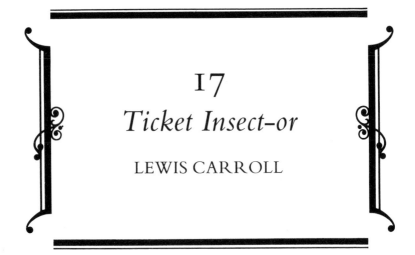

17

Ticket Insect-or

LEWIS CARROLL

'Tickets, please!' said the Guard, putting his head in at the window. In a moment everybody was holding out a ticket: they were about the same size as the people, and quite seemed to fill the carriage.

'Now then! Show your ticket, child!' the Guard went on, looking angrily at Alice. And a great many voices all said together ('like the chorus of a song,' thought Alice), 'Don't keep him waiting, child! Why, his time is worth a thousand pounds a minute!'

'I'm afraid I haven't got one,' Alice said in a frightened tone: 'there wasn't a ticket office where I came from.' And again the chorus of voices went on, 'There wasn't room for one where she came from. The land there is worth a thousand pounds an inch!'

'Don't make excuses,' said the Guard: 'you should have bought one from the engine driver,' and once more the chorus of voices went on with 'The man that drives the engine. Why, the smoke alone is worth a thousand pounds a puff!'

Alice thought to herself, 'Then there's no use in speaking.' The voices didn't join in this time, as she hadn't spoken, but, to her great surprise, they all thought in chorus (I hope you understand what *thinking in chorus* means—for I must confess that *I* don't), 'Better say nothing at all. Language is worth a thousand pounds a word!'

'I shall dream about a thousand pounds tonight, I know I shall!' thought Alice.

All this time the Guard was looking at her, first through a telescope, then through a microscope, and then through an opera-glass. At last he said, 'You're travelling the wrong way,' and shut up the window and went away.

'So young a child,' said the gentleman sitting opposite to her (he was dressed in white paper), 'ought to know which way she's going, even if she doesn't know her own name!'

A Goat, that was sitting next to the gentleman in white, shut his eyes and said in a loud voice, 'She ought to know her way to the ticket office, even if she doesn't know her alphabet!'

There was a Beetle sitting next the Goat (it was a very queer set of passengers altogether), and, as the rule seemed to be that they should all speak in turn, *he* went on with 'She'll have to go back from here as luggage!'

Alice couldn't see who was sitting beyond the Beetle, but a hoarse voice spoke next. 'Change engines—' it said, and there it choked and was obliged to leave off.

'It sounds like a horse,' Alice thought to herself. And an extremely small voice, close to her ear, said, 'You might make a joke on that—something about "horse and "hoarse", you know.'

Then a very gentle voice in the distance said, 'She must be labelled "Lass, with care", you know—'

And after that other voices went on ('What a number of people there are in the carriage!' thought Alice), saying, 'She must go by post, as she's got a head on her—' 'She must be sent as a message by the telegraph—' 'She must draw the train herself the rest of the way—' and so on.

But the gentleman dressed in white paper leaned forwards and whispered in her ear, 'Never mind what they all say, my dear, but take a return-ticket every time the train stops.'

'Indeed I shan't!' Alice said rather impatiently. 'I don't belong to this railway journey at all—I was in a wood just now—and I wish I could get back there!' 'You might make a joke on *that*,' said the little voice close to her ear: 'something about "you *would*, if you could", you know.'

'Don't tease so,' said Alice, looking about in vain to see where the voice came from; 'if you're so anxious to have a joke made, why don't you make one yourself?'

The little voice sighed deeply: it was *very* unhappy, evidently, and Alice would have said something pitying to comfort it, 'if it would only sigh like other people!' she thought. But this was such a wonderfully small sigh, that she wouldn't have heard it at all, if it hadn't come *quite* close to her ear. The consequence of this was that it tickled her ear very much, and *quite* took off her thoughts from the unhappiness of the poor little creature.

'I know you are a friend,'the little voice went on; 'a dear friend, and an old friend. And you won't hurt me, though I *am* an insect.'

'What kind of insect?' Alice inquired a little anxiously. What she really wanted to know was, whether it could sting or not, but she thought this wouldn't be quite a civil question to ask.

'What, then you don't—' the little voice began, when it was drowned by a shrill scream from the engine, and everybody jumped up in alarm, Alice among the rest.

The Horse, who had put his head out of the window, quietly drew it in and said, 'It's only a brook we have to jump over.' Everybody seemed satisfied with this, though Alice felt a little nervous at the idea of trains jumping at all. 'However, it'll take us into the Fourth Square, that's some comfort!' she said to herself. In another moment she felt the carriage rise straight up into the air, and in her fright she caught at the thing nearest to her hand, which happened to be the Goat's beard.

18

The Engine-Burglar

E. NESBIT

The very next morning Bobbie began to watch her oppor-
tunity to get Peter's engine mended secretly. And the op-
portunity came the very next afternoon.

Mother went by train to the nearest town to do shopping.
When she went there, she always went to the Post Office.
Perhaps to post her letters to Father, for she never gave them
to the children or Mrs Viney to post, and she never went to
the village herself. Peter and Phyllis went with her. Bobbie
wanted an excuse not to go, but try as she would she couldn't
think of a good one. And just when she felt that all was lost,
her frock caught on a big nail by the kitchen door and there
was a great criss-cross tear all along the front of the skirt. I
assure you this was really an accident. So the others pitied
her and went without her, for there was no time for her to
change, because they were rather late already and had to
hurry to the station to catch the train.

When they had gone, Bobbie put on her everyday frock,
and went down to the railway. She did not go into the
station, but she went along the line to the end of the platform
where the engine is when the down train is alongside the
platform—the place where there are a water tank and a long,
limp, leather hose, like an elephant's trunk. She hid behind
a bush on the other side of the railway. She had the toy
engine done up in brown paper, and she waited patiently
with it under her arm.

Then when the next train came in and stopped, Bobbie went across the metals of the up line and stood beside the engine. She had never been so close to an engine before. It looked much larger and harder than she had expected, and it made her feel very small indeed, and, somehow, very soft—as if she could very, very easily be hurt rather badly.

'I know what silkworms feel like now,' said Bobbie to herself.

The engine driver and fireman did not see her. They were leaning out of the other side, telling the Porter a tale about a dog and a leg of mutton.

'If you please,' said Roberta —but the engine was blowing off steam and no one heard her.

'If you please, Mr Engineer,' she spoke a little louder, but the engine happened to speak at the same moment, and of course Roberta's soft little voice hadn't a chance.

It seemed to her that the only way would be to climb on to the engine and pull at their coats. The step was high, but she got her knee on it, and clambered into the cab; she stumbled and fell on hands and knees on the base of the great heap of coals that led up to the square opening in the tender. The engine was not above the weaknesses of its fellows; it was making a great deal more noise than there was the slightest need for. And just as Roberta fell on the coals, the engine driver, who had turned without seeing her, started the engine, and when Bobbie had picked herself up, the train was moving—not fast, but much too fast for her to get off.

All sorts of dreadful thoughts came to her all together in one horrible flash. There were such things as express trains which went on, she supposed, for hundreds of miles without stopping. Suppose this should be one of them? How would she get home again? She had no money to pay for the return journey.

'And I've no business here. I'm an engine-burglar—that's what I am,' she thought. 'I shouldn't wonder if they could lock me up for this.' And the train was going faster and faster.

There was something in her throat that made it impossible for her to speak. She tried twice. The men had their backs to her. They were doing something to things that looked like taps.

Suddenly she put out her hand and caught hold of the nearest sleeve. The man turned with a start, and he and Roberta stood for a minute looking at each other in silence. Then the silence was broken by them both.

The man said, 'Here's a bloomin' go!' and Roberta burst into tears.

The other man said he was blooming well blest—or something like it—but though naturally surprised they were not exactly unkind.

'You're a naughty little girl, that's what you are,' said the fireman, but the engine driver said:

'Darling little piece, I call her,' but they made her sit down on an iron seat in the cab and told her to stop crying and tell them what she meant by it.

She did stop, as soon as she could. One thing that helped her was the thought that Peter would give almost his ears to be in her place—on a real engine—really going. The children had often wondered whether any engine driver could be found noble enough to take them for a ride on an engine— and now here she was. She dried her eyes and sniffed earnestly.

'Now, then,' said the fireman, 'out with it. What do you mean by it, eh?'

'Oh please, ' sniffed Bobbie, and stopped.

'Try again,' said the engine driver, encouragingly.

Bobbie tried again.

'Please, Mr Engineer,' she said, 'I did call out to you from the line, but you didn't hear me—and I just climbed up to touch you on the arm—quite gently I meant to do it—and then I fell into the coals—and I am so sorry if I frightened you. Oh, don't be cross—oh, please don't!' She sniffed again.

'We ain't so much *cross*,' said the fireman, 'as interested like. It ain't every day a little gel tumbles into our coal bunker outer the sky, is it, Bill? What did you *do* it for—eh?'

'That's the point,' agreed the engine driver; 'what did you do it *for*?'

Bobbie found that she had not quite stopped crying. The engine driver patted her on the back and said: 'Here, cheer up, Mate. It ain't so bad as all that 'ere, I'll be bound.'

'I wanted,' said Bobbie, much cheered to find herself addressed as 'Mate'—'I only wanted to ask you if you'd be so kind as to mend this.' She picked up the brown-paper parcel from among the coals and undid the string with hot, red fingers that trembled.

Her feet and legs felt the scorch of the engine fire, but her shoulders felt the wild chill rush of the air. The engine lurched and shook and rattled, and as they shot under a bridge the engine seemed to shout in her ears.

The fireman shovelled on coals.

Bobbie unrolled the brown paper and disclosed the toy engine.

'I thought,' she said wistfully, 'that perhaps you'd mend this for me—because you're an engineer, you know.'

The engine driver said he was blowed if he wasn't blest.

'I'm blest if I ain't blowed,' remarked the fireman.

But the engine driver took the little engine and looked at it—and the fireman ceased for an instant to shovel coal, and looked, too.

'It's like your precious cheek,' said the engine driver—'whatever made you think we'd be bothered tinkering penny toys?'

'I didn't mean it for precious cheek,' said Bobbie; 'only everybody that has anything to do with railways is so kind and good. I didn't think you'd mind. You don't really—do you?' she added, for she had seen a not unkindly wink pass between the two.

'My trade's driving of a engine, not mending her—especially such a hout-size in engines as this 'ere,' said Bill. 'An' 'ow are we a-goin' to get you back to your sorrowing friends and relations, and all be forgiven and forgotten?'

'If you'll put me down next time you stop,' said Bobbie, firmly, though her heart beat fiercely against her arm as she clasped her hands, 'and lend me the money for a third-class ticket, I'll pay you back—honour bright. I'm not a confidence trick like in the newspapers—really, I'm not.'

'You're a little lady, every inch,' said Bill, relenting suddenly and completely. 'We'll see you get home safe. An' about this engine—Jim—ain't you got ne'er a pal as can use a soldering iron? Seems to me that's about all the little bounder wants doing to it.'

'That's what Father said,' Bobbie explained eagerly. 'What's that for?'

She pointed to a little brass wheel that he had turned as he spoke.

'That's the injector.'

'In—what?'

'Injector to fill up the boiler.'

'Oh,' said Bobbie, mentally registering the fact to tell the others; 'that is interesting.'

'This 'ere's the automatic brake,' Bill went on, flattered by her enthusiasm. 'You just move this 'ere little handle—do it with one finger, you can—and the train jolly soon stops. That's what they call the Power of Science in the newpapers.'

He showed her two little dials, like clock faces, and told her how one showed how much steam was going, and the other showed if the brake was working properly.

By the time she had seen him shut off steam with a big shining steel handle, Bobbie knew more about the inside working of an engine than she had ever thought there was to know, and Jim had promised that his second cousin's wife's brother should solder the toy engine, or Jim would know the reason why. Besides all the knowledge she had gained Bobbie felt that she and Bill and Jim were now friends for life, and that they had wholly and forever forgiven her for stumbling uninvited among the sacred coals of their tender.

At Stacklepoole Junction she parted from them with warm expressions of mutual regard. They handed her over to the guard of a returning train—a friend of theirs—and she had the joy of knowing what guards do in their secret fastnesses, and understood how when you pull the communication cord in railway carriages, a wheel goes round under the guard's nose and a loud bell rings in his ears. She asked the guard why his van smelt so fishy, and learned that he had to carry a lot of fish every day, and that the wetness in the hollows of the corrugated floor had all drained out of the boxes full of plaice and cod and mackerel and soles and smelts.

Bobbie got home in time for tea, and she felt as though her mind would burst with all that had been put into it since she parted from the others. How she blessed the nail that had torn her frock!

'Where have you been?' asked the others.

'To the station of course,' said Roberta. But she would not tell a word of her adventures till the day appointed, when she mysteriously led them to the station at the hour of 3.19's transit, and proudly introduced them to her friends, Bill and Jim. Jim's second cousin's wife's brother had not been unworthy of the sacred trust imposed in him. The toy engine was, literally, as good as new.

'Goodbye—oh, goodbye,' said Bobbie, just before the engine screamed *its* goodbye. 'I shall always, always love you —and Jim's second cousin's wife's brother as well!'

And as the three children went home up the hill, Peter hugging the engine, now quite its old self again, Bobbie told, with joyous leaps of the heart, the story of how she had been an Engine-burglar.

19

The Story-Teller

SAKI

It was a hot afternoon, and the railway carriage was correspondingly sultry, and the next stop was at Templecombe, nearly an hour ahead. The occupants of the carriage were a small girl, and a smaller girl, and a small boy. An aunt belonging to the children occupied one corner seat, and the further corner seat on the opposite side was occupied by a bachelor who was a stranger to their party, but the small girls and the small boy emphatically occupied the compartment. Both the aunt and the children were conversational in a limited, persistent way, reminding one of the attentions of a house-fly that refused to be discouraged. Most of the aunt's remarks seemed to begin with 'Don't,' and nearly all of the children's remarks began with 'Why?' The bachelor said nothing out loud.

'Don't Cyril, don't,' exclaimed the aunt, as the small boy began smacking the cushions of the seat, producing a cloud of dust at each blow.

'Come and look out of the window,' she added.

The child moved reluctantly to the window. 'Why are those sheep being driven out of that field?' he asked.

'I expect they are being driven to another field where there is more grass,' said the aunt weakly.

'But there is lots of grass in that field,' protested the boy; 'there's nothing else but grass there. Aunt, there's lots of grass in that field.'

'Perhaps the grass in the other field is better,' suggested the aunt fatuously.

'Why is it better?' came the swift, inevitable question.

'Oh, look at those cows!' exclaimed the aunt. Nearly every field along the line had contained cows or bullocks, but she spoke as though she were drawing attention to a rarity.

'Why is the grass in the other field better?' persisted Cyril.

The frown on the bachelor's face was deepening to a scowl. He was a hard, unsympathetic man, the aunt decided in her mind. She was utterly unable to come to any satisfactory decision about the grass in the other field.

The smaller girl created a diversion by beginning to recite 'On the Road to Mandalay.' She only knew the first line, but she put her limited knowledge to the fullest possible use. She repeated the line over and over again in a dreamy but resolute and very audible voice; it seemed to the bachelor as though someone had had a bet with her that she could not repeat the line aloud two thousand times without stopping. Whoever it was who had made the wager was likely to lose his bet.

'Come over here and listen to a story,' said the aunt, when the bachelor had looked twice at her and once at the communication cord.

The children moved listlessly towards the aunt's end of the carriage. Evidently her reputation as a story-teller did not rank high in their estimation.

In a low, confidential voice, interrupted at frequent intervals by loud, petulant questions from her listeners, she began an unenterprising and deplorably uninteresting story about a little girl who was good, and made friends with every one on account of her goodness, and was finally saved from a mad bull by a number of rescuers who admired her moral character.

'Wouldn't they have saved her if she hadn't been good?' demanded the bigger of the small girls. It was exactly the question that the bachelor had wanted to ask.

'Well, yes,' admitted the aunt lamely, 'but I don't think they would have run quite so fast to her help if they had not liked her so much.'

'It's the stupidest story I've ever heard,' said the bigger of the small girls, with immense conviction.

'I didn't listen after the first bit, it was so stupid,' said Cyril.

The smaller girl made no actual comment on the story, but she had long ago recommenced a murmured repetition of her favourite line.

'You don't seem to be a success as a story-teller,' said the bachelor suddenly from his corner.

The aunt bristled in instant defence at this unexpected attack.

'It's a very difficult thing to tell stories that children can both understand and appreciate,' she said stiffly.

'I don't agree with you,' said the bachelor.

'Perhaps *you* would like to tell them a story,' was the aunt's retort.

'Tell us a story,' demanded the bigger of the small girls.

'Once upon a time,' began the bachelor, 'there was a little girl called Bertha, who was extraordinarily good.'

The children's momentarily-aroused interest began at once to flicker; all stories seemed dreadfully alike, no matter who told them.

'She did all that she was told, she was always truthful, she kept her clothes clean, ate milk puddings as though they were jam tarts, learned her lessons perfectly, and was polite in her manners.'

'Was she pretty?' asked the bigger of the small girls.

'Not as pretty as any of you,' said the bachelor, 'but she was horribly good.'

There was a wave of reaction in favour of the story; the word horrible in connection with goodness was a novelty that commended itself. It seemed to introduce a ring of truth that was absent from the aunt's tale of infant life.

'She was so good,' continued the bachelor, 'that she won several medals for goodness, which she always wore, pinned on to her dress. There was a medal for obedience, another medal for punctuality, and a third for good behaviour. They were large metal medals and they clinked against one another as she walked. No other child in the town where she lived had as many as three medals, so everybody knew that she must be an extra good child.'

'Horribly good,' quoted Cyril.

'Everybody talked about her goodness, and the Prince of

the country got to hear about it, and he said that as she was so very good she might be allowed once a week to walk in his park, which was just outside the town. It was a beautiful park, and no children were ever allowed in it, so it was a great honour for Bertha to be allowed to go there.'

'Were there any sheep in the park?' demanded Cyril.

'No,' said the bachelor, 'there were no sheep.'

'Why weren't there any sheep?' came the inevitable question arising out of that answer.

The aunt permitted herself a smile, which might almost have been described as a grin.

'There were no sheep in the park,' said the bachelor, 'because the Prince's mother had once had a dream that her son would either be killed by a sheep or else by a clock falling on him. For that reason the Prince never kept a sheep in his park or a clock in his palace.'

The aunt suppressed a gasp of admiration.

'Was the Prince killed by a sheep or by a clock?' asked Cyril.

'He is still alive, so we can't tell whether the dream will come true,' said the bachelor unconcernedly; 'anyway, there were no sheep in the park, but there were lots of little pigs running all over the place.'

'What colour were they?'

'Black with white faces, white with black spots, black all over, grey with white patches, and some were white all over.'

The story-teller paused to let a full idea of the park's treasures sink into the children's imaginations; then he resumed:

'Bertha was rather sorry to find that there were no flowers in the park. She had promised her aunts, with tears in her eyes, that she would not pick any of the kind Prince's flowers, and she had meant to keep her promise, so of course it made her feel silly to find that there were no flowers to pick.'

'Why weren't there any flowers?'

'Because the pigs had eaten them all,' said the bachelor promptly. 'The gardeners had told the Prince that you couldn't have pigs and flowers, so he decided to have pigs and no flowers.'

There was a murmur of approval at the excellence of the

Prince's decision; so many people would have decided the other way.

'There were lots of other delightful things in the park. There were ponds with gold and blue and green fish in them, and trees with beautiful parrots that said clever things at a moment's notice, and humming birds that hummed all the popular tunes of the day. Bertha walked up and down and enjoyed herself immensely, and thought to herself: "If I were not so extraordinarily good I should not have been allowed to come into this beautiful park and enjoy all that there is to be seen in it," and her three medals clinked against one another as she walked and helped to remind her how very good she really was. Just then an enormous wolf came prowling into the park to see if it could catch a fat little pig for its supper.'

'What colour was it?' asked the children, amid an immediate quickening of interest.

'Mud-colour all over, with a black tongue and pale grey eyes that gleamed with unspeakable ferocity. The first thing that it saw in the park was Bertha; her pinafore was so spotlessly white and clean that it could be seen from a great distance. Bertha saw the wolf and saw that it was stealing towards her, and she began to wish that she had never been allowed to come into the park. She ran as hard as she could, and the wolf came after her with huge leaps and bounds. She managed to reach a shrubbery of myrtle bushes and she hid herself in one of the thickest of the bushes. The wolf came sniffing among the branches, its black tongue lolling out of its mouth and its pale grey eyes glaring with rage. Bertha was terribly frightened, and thought to herself: "If I had not been so extraordinarily good I should have been safe in the town at this moment." However, the scent of the myrtle was so strong that the wolf could not sniff out where Bertha was hiding, and the bushes were so thick that he might have hunted about in them for a long time without catching sight of her, so he thought he might as well go off and catch a little pig instead. Bertha was trembling very much at having the wolf prowling and sniffing so near her, and as she trembled the medal for obedience clinked against the medals for good conduct and punctuality. The wolf was just moving away when he heard the sound of the medals clinking and stopped to listen; they clinked again in a bush quite near him. He dashed into the bush, his pale grey eyes gleaming with ferocity and triumph, and dragged Bertha out and devoured her to the last morsel. All that was left of her were her shoes, bits of clothing, and the three medals for goodness.'

'Were any of the little pigs killed?'

'No, they all escaped.'

'The story began badly,' said the smaller of the small girls, 'but it had a beautiful ending.'

'It is the most beautiful story that I ever heard,' said the bigger of the small girls, with immense decision.

'It is the *only* beautiful story I have ever heard,' said Cyril.

A dissentient opinion came from the aunt.

'A most improper story to tell to young children! You have undermined the effect of years of careful teaching.'

'At any rate,' said the bachelor, collecting his belongings preparatory to leaving the carriage, 'I kept them quiet for ten minutes, which was more than you were able to do.'

'Unhappy woman!' he observed to himself as he walked down the platform of Templecombe station; 'for the next six months or so those children will assail her in public with demands for an improper story!'

V

WAR AND PEACE

*On the whole I adhere to the view I expressed in a kind
of Ode to Steamrollers (in 1955):*

   *'Steam, so Victorian, like Carlyle or Tennyson,
   Unlike most inventions, was always a benison.'*

*Perhaps the very nature of most people's cosy domestic
picture of railways makes 'armoured trains', those di-
nosaurs of warfare, let alone the appalling death trains
of Hitler's Germany, seem even more awful by compar-
ison. Peter Fleming's piece on war-torn Greece brings
back the memory of that very brave and marvellously
witty man's voice. Auden is in at the birth of the
documentary film, Georgian Monro makes the same yet
a different journey, Evoe's Percy is indeed Everlasting.
And everlasting, too, thank goodness, is J. B. Priestley
—and how gratifying to discover a shared feeling about
those railway amnesiacs.*

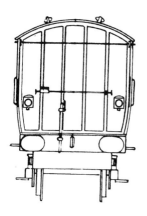

20

Ammunition Train

PETER FLEMING

I forget which of us it was who found the ammunition train. There were two of them, as a matter of fact, lying forlornly in a railway siding outside the town of Larissa. Larissa in the great empty plain of Thessaly was (the) main supply base in Northern Greece from which, in April 1941, the British Expeditionary forces were withdrawing under heavy German pressure.

The town had been bombed by the Italians, then it had been badly damaged by an earthquake, and now it was receiving regular attention from the Luftwaffe. It was an awful mess. The Greek railway staff had run away, and it was pretty obvious that the two ammunition trains had been abandoned. I knew that we were seriously short of ammunition further down the line so I went to the Brigadier in charge of the base and asked permission to try and get one of the trains away. It was given with alacrity.

I don't want you to think that this action on my part was public-spirited, or anything like that. My motives were purely selfish. *We wanted a job.* We were a small unit which had been carrying out various irregular activities further north; but now the sort of tasks for which we were designed had become impossible, and we were in danger of becoming what Civil Servants call redundant. We felt that if we could get this train away we should be doing something useful and justifying our existence. Besides, one of us claimed that he knew how to drive an engine.

This was Norman Johnstone, a brother officer in the Grenadier Guards. One of our jobs earlier in the campaign had been to destroy some rolling-stock which could not be moved away. Norman had a splendid time blowing up about twenty valuable locomotives and a lot of trucks, but towards the end we ran out of explosives. At this stage a sergeant in the 4th Hussars turned up, who was an engine driver in civilian life. With Norman helping him, he got steam up in the four surviving engines, drove them a quarter of a mile down the line, then sent them full tilt back into the station where they caused further havoc of a spectacular and enjoyable kind.

These were perhaps not ideal conditions under which to learn how to drive an engine, especially as the whole thing was carried out under shell-fire; and all we really knew for certain about Norman's capabilities as an engine driver was that every single locomotive with which he had been associated had become scrap metal in a matter of minutes. Still, he was a very determined and a very methodical chap, and there seemed no harm in letting him have a go. So early in the morning we made our way to the railway station, just in time for the first air raid of the day.

Except for occasional parties of refugees and stragglers from the Greek army the station was deserted. There were two excellent reasons for this. First of all there were no trains running, so there was no point in anybody going there anyhow. Secondly, the station was practically the only thing left in the ruins of Larissa that was worth bombing; we had ten air raids altogether before we left in the afternoon, and they always had a go at the station.

The first thing we had to do was to get steam up in a railway engine. There were plenty of these about but all except two had been rendered unserviceable by the Luftwaffe. We started work on the bigger of the two.

After having a quick look round Norman explained to us that one of the most popular—and probably in the long run the *soundest*—of all methods of making steam was by boiling water; but we, he said, might have to devise some alternative formula, as the water mains had been cut by bombs and there was very little coal to be found. However, in the long run we got together enough of these two more or less essential ingredients, and all was going well when one of the few large bombs that came our way blew a hole in the track just outside the shed we were working in—thus, as it were, locking the stable door before we had been able to steal the horse. Greatly disgusted, we transferred our attention to the only other sound engine.

There were more air raids, and it came on to rain, and two Greek deserters stole my car, and altogether things did not look very hopeful, especially when somebody pointed out that there was now only one undamaged and navigable set of tracks leading out of the battered marshalling-yard.

But the needle on the pressure-gauge in the cabin of our engine was rising slowly, and at last, whistling excitedly, the ancient machine got under way. It was a majestic sight, and it would have been even more majestic if she had not gone backwards instead of forwards.

It was at this point that a certain gap in Norman's education as an engine driver became evident. The sergeant in the 4th Hussars had taught him how to start a locomotive and how to launch it on a career of self-destruction; but Norman's early training in how to stop an engine had been confined entirely to making it run violently into a lot of other rolling-stock. We trotted anxiously along the cinders, hanging, so to speak, on to Norman's stirrup leathers. 'Do you know how to stop?' we shouted. 'Not yet,' replied Norman, a trifle testily.

But he soon found out and presently mastered the knack of making the engine go forwards as well as backwards, and we steamed rather incredulously northwards towards the siding where the ammunition trains lay.

We chose the bigger of the two. It consisted of twenty-six trucks containing one hundred and twenty tons of ammunition and one hundred and fifty tons of petrol. It was not what you might call an ideally balanced cargo from our point of view, and nobody particularly wanted the petrol, but the train was made up like that and we had to lump it. . . .

Almost as soon as we had left Larissa we began to climb up a long, gentle slope; and we had only done about five miles when the needle on the pressure-gauge began slowly but firmly to fall. We stoked like mad. Norman pulled, pushed and twiddled the various devices on what we quite incorrectly called the dashboard. Pressure continued to fall, and the train went slower and slower. At last it stopped altogether.

'We'd better get out,' said Norman, 'and have a look at the injector-sprockets.' He may not actually have said 'injector-sprockets' but anyhow it was some technical term which meant nothing to us and may not have meant a very great deal to him. It was at this point that we realised that the train was not merely stopped but was beginning to run slowly backwards down the hill. The thought of free-wheeling backwards into Larissa was distasteful to all of us. In the hurry of departure we had had no time to organise our ten brakemen, who were confined in the guard's van instead of being dispersed along the train so that they could operate the brakes on individual goods wagons.

There was only one thing to do. I leapt off the engine and ran back down the train as fast as I could, like an old lady running for a bus, jumped on the back of the nearest goods van, swarmed up a little ladder on to its roof and feverishly turned the wheel which put the brake on. The train continued to go backwards, but it seemed to have stopped gathering speed and at last, after I had repeated this operation several times, it came reluctantly to a stop.

We were really getting a great deal of fun out of this train. We had got a tremendous kick out of starting it, and now we were scarcely less elated at having brought it to a standstill. But we had to face the facts and the *main* fact was that as engine drivers, though we had no doubt some excellent qualities—originality, determination, cheerfulness and so on—we were open to the serious criticism that we didn't seem to be able to drive our engine very far. A run of five miles, with a small discount for going backwards unexpectedly, is not much to show for a hard day's work.

At this point, moreover, it suddenly began to look as if we were going to lose our precious train altogether. As we tinkered away at the engine, the air grew loud with an expected but none the less unwelcome noise, and a number of enemy bombers could be seen marching through the sky towards us. We were a very conspicuous object in the middle of that empty plain and I quickly gave orders for the ten men in the guard's van to go and take cover five hundred yards from the train. In point of fact there was no cover to take but they trotted off with alacrity and sat down round a small tree about the size of a big gooseberry bush in the middle distance. We could not very well leave the engine because the fire might have gone out (or anyhow we thought it might) and we should have had to start all over again.

But if we had our troubles the enemy, as so often happens, had his too. The bombers were obviously interested in us, but it soon became equally obvious that they had no bombs, having wasted them all on the ruins of Larissa earlier in the day.

They still, however, had their machine-guns and three or four of the aircraft proceeded to attack us, coming in very low one after the other. But they all made the same mistake, which they might not have made if we ourselves had taken evasive action and left the train. They all attacked the engine, round which they could see signs of life, instead of flying up and down the twenty odd wagons full of petrol and H.E. and spraying them with bullets, which could hardly have failed to produce spectacular results. They concentrated on putting the engine out of action; and the engine, as we ourselves were just beginning to realise, was out of action already, all the water in the boiler having somehow disappeared.

We used the engine in much the same way as one uses a grouse-butt. Whichever side the attack was coming from, we got the other side. The flying machine, making a terrible noise and blazing away with its machine-gun, swept down on us and as it roared overhead—much bigger, much more malevolent but not really very much *higher* than the average grouse—we pooped off at it with our tommy-gun, to which the German rear-gunner replied with a burst that kicked up the dust a hundred yards away or more. It got rather silly after a bit. I am quite sure we never hit the Luftwaffe, and the only damage the Luftwaffe did to us was to make a hole in a map somebody had left in the cab. And one of the things about driving a train is that you do not need a map to do it with.

They gave it up quite soon—it was getting late anyhow—

and went home to Bulgaria. We climbed back into our engine again, and as I looked at our only casualty—the map, torn by an explosive bullet and covered in coal dust—I could not help rather envying the Luftwaffe who believed that they had succeeded in doing what they set out to do. It was only too obvious that we had not. Night fell and it was fairly cold.

Then all of a sudden, out of the darkness, another train appeared, full of Australian gunners whose guns were supposed to have come on the road. They towed us back to the next station. Here we picked up a good engine with a Greek driver and set off for the south.

Forty-eight hours after we had started work on this unlikely project we reached our—or rather the ammunition's—destination. It was a place called Amphykleion and here I formally handed over the train—twenty-six coaches, one hundred and fifty tons of petrol, one hundred and twenty tons of ammunition—to the supply people. Everyone was delighted with it. 'This really will make a difference,' they said. We felt childishly pleased. The sun shone, it was a lovely morning. And this marked improvement in the weather made it comparatively easy for a small force of German dive-bombers, a few hours later, to dispose of the train and all its contents with a terrible finality.

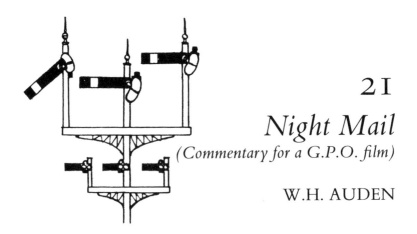

21

Night Mail

(Commentary for a G.P.O. film)

W.H. AUDEN

This is the Night Mail crossing the Border,
Bringing the cheque and the postal order,
Letters for the rich, letters for the poor,
The shop at the corner and the girl next door.
Pulling up Beattock, a steady climb:
The gradient's against her but she's on time.

Past cotton grass and moorland boulder,
Shovelling white steam over her shoulder,
Snorting noisily as she passes
Silent miles of wind-bent grasses.
Birds turn their heads as she approaches,
Stare from the bushes at her blank-faced coaches.
Sheepdogs cannot turn her course;
They slumber on with paws across.
In the farm she passes no one wakes,
But a jug in a bedroom gently shakes.

Dawn freshens, the climb is done.
Down towards Glasgow she descends,
Towards the steam tugs, yelping down the glade of
    cranes,
Towards the fields of apparatus, the furnaces
Set on the dark plain like gigantic chessmen.
All Scotland waits for her:
In the dark glens, beside the pale-green sea lochs,
Men long for news.

Letters of thanks, letters from banks,
Letters of joy from the girl and boy,
Receipted bills and invitations
To inspect new stock or visit relations,
And applications for situations,
And timid lovers' declarations,
And gossip, gossip from all the nations,
News circumstantial, news financial,
Letters with holiday snaps to enlarge in,
Letters with faces scrawled in the margin,
Letters from uncles, cousins and aunts,
Letters to Scotland from the South of France,
Letters of condolence to Highlands and Lowlands,
Notes from overseas to the Hebrides;
Written on paper of every hue,
The pink, the violet, the white and the blue,
The chatty, the catty, the boring, adoring,
The cold and official and the heart's outpouring,
Clever, stupid, short and long,
The typed and the printed and the spelt all wrong.

Thousands are still asleep,
Dreaming of terrifying monsters
Or a friendly tea beside the band at Cranston's or
    Crawford's:
Asleep in working Glasgow, asleep in well-set
    Edinburgh,
Asleep in granite Aberdeen,
They continue their dreams,
But shall wake soon and long for letters,
And none will hear the postman's knock
Without a quickening of the heart.
For who can bear to feel himself forgotten?

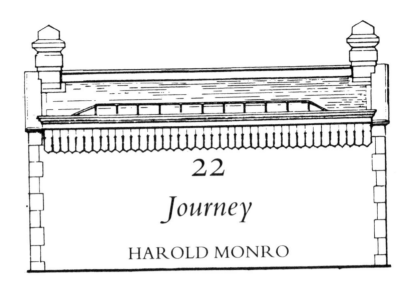

22

Journey

HAROLD MONRO

How many times I nearly miss the train
By running up the staircase once again
For some dear trifle almost left behind.
At that last moment the unwary mind
Forgets the solemn tick of station-time;
That muddy lane the feet must climb—
The bridge—the ticket—signal down—
Train just emerging beyond the town:
The great blue engine panting as it takes
The final curve, and grinding on its brakes
Up to the platform-edge ... The little doors
Swing open, while the burly porter roars.
The tight compartment fills: our careful eyes
Go to explore each other's destinies.
A lull. The station master waves. The train
Gathers, and grips, and takes the rails again,
Moves to the shining open land, and soon
Begins to tittle-tattle a tame tattoon.

They ramble through the countryside,
Dear gentle monsters, and we ride
Pleasantly seated—so we sink
Into a torpor on the brink
Of thought, or read our books, and understand
Half them and half the backward-gliding land:

(Trees in a dance all twirling round;
Large rivers flowing with no sound;
The scattered images of town and field,
Shining flowers half concealed.)
And, having settled to an equal rate,
They swing the curve and straighten to the straight,
Curtail their stride and gather up their joints,
Snort, dwindle their steam for the noisy points,
Leap them in safety, and, the other side,
Loop again to an even stride.

The long train moves: we move in it along.
Like an old ballad, or an endless song,
It drones and wimbles its unwearied croon—
Croons, drones, and mumbles all the afternoon.

Towns with their fifty chimneys close and high,
Wreathed in great smoke between the earth and sky,
It hurtles through them, and you think it must
Halt—but it shrieks and sputters them with dust,
Cracks like a bullet through their big affairs,
Rushes the station-bridge, and disappears
Out to the suburb, laying bare
Each garden trimmed with pitiful care;
Children are caught at idle play,
Held a moment, and thrown away.
Nearly everyone looks round.
Some dignified inhabitant is found
Right in the middle of the commonplace—
Buttoning his trousers, or washing his face.

Oh the wild engine! Every time I sit
In any train I must remember it.
The way it smashes through the air; its great
Petulant majesty and terrible rate:
Driving the ground before it, with those round
Feet pounding, eating, covering the ground;
The piston using up the white steam so
You cannot watch it when it come or go;
The cutting, the embankment; how it takes
The tunnels, and the clatter that it makes;

So careful of the train and of the track,
Guiding us out, or helping us go back;
Breasting its destination: at the close
Yawning, and slowly dropping to a doze.

We who have looked each other in the eyes
This journey long, and trundled with the train,
Now to our separate purposes must rise,
Becoming decent strangers once again.
The little chamber we have made our home
In which we so conveniently abode,
The complicated journey we have come,
Must be an unremembered episode.
Our common purpose made us all like friends.
How suddenly it ends!
A nod, a murmur, or a little smile,
Or often nothing, and away we file.
I hate to leave you, comrades. I will stay
To watch you drift apart and pass away.
It seems impossible to go and meet
All those strange eyes of people in the street.
But, like some proud unconscious god, the train
Gathers us up and scatters us again.

23

The Everlasting Percy

E.V. KNOX
(EVOE)

I used to be a fearful lad,
The things I did were downright bad;
And worst of all were what I done
From seventeen to twenty-one
On all the railways far and wide
From sinfulness and shameful pride.

For several years I was so wicked
I used to go without a ticket,
And travelled underneath the seat
Down in the dust of people's feet,
Or else I sat as bold as brass
And told them 'Season', in first-class.
In 1921, at Harwich,
I smoked in a non-smoking carriage;
I never knew what Life nor Art meant,
I wrote 'Reserved' on my compartment,
And once (I was a guilty man)
I swopped the labels in guard's van.

From 1922 to 4
I leant against the carriage door
Without a-looking at the latch;
And once, a-leaving Colney Hatch,
I put a huge and heavy parcel
Which I were taking to Newcastle,
Entirely filled with lumps of lead,
Up on the rack above my head;
And when it tumbled down, oh Lord!
I pulled communication cord.
The guard came round and said, 'You mule!
What have you done, you dirty fool?'
I simply sat and smiled, and said
'Is this train right for Holyhead?'
He said 'You blinking blasted swine,
You'll have to pay the five-pound fine.'
I gave a false name and address,
Puffed up with my vaingloriousness.

At Bickershaw and Strood and Staines
I've often got on moving trains,
And once alit at Norwood West
Before my coach had come to rest.
A window and a lamp I broke
At Chipping Sodbury and Stoke,
And worse I did at Wissendine:
I threw out bottles on the line
And other articles as be
Likely to cause grave injury
To persons working on the line—
That's what I did at Wissendine.
I grew so careless what I'd do
Throwing things out, and dangerous too,
That, last and worst of all I'd done,
I threw a great sultana bun
Out of the train at Pontypridd—
It hit a platelayer, it did.
I thought that I should have to swing
And never hear the sweet birds sing.
The jury recommended mercy,
And that's how grace was given to Percy. . . .

24
On Travel by Train

J.B. PRIESTLEY

Remove an Englishman from his hearth and home, his centre of corporal life, and he becomes a very different creature, one capable of sudden furies and roaring passions, a deep sea of strong emotions churning beneath his frozen exterior. I can pass, at all times, for a quiet, neighbourly fellow, yet have I sat, more than once, in a railway carriage with black murder in my heart. At the mere sight of some probably inoffensive fellow-passenger my whole being will be invaded by a million devils of wrath, and I 'could do such bitter business as the day would quake to look on'.

There is one type of traveller that never fails to rouse my quick hatred. She is a large, middle-aged woman, with a rasping voice and a face of brass. Above all things, she loves to invade smoking compartments that are already comfortably filled with a quiet company of smokers; she will come bustling in, shouting over her shoulder at her last victim, a prostrate porter, and, laden with packages of all maddening shapes and sizes, she will glare defiantly about her until some unfortunate has given up his seat. She is often accompanied by some sort of contemptible, whining cur that is only one degree less offensive than its mistress. From the moment that she has wedged herself in there will be no more peace in the carriage, but simmering hatred, and everywhere dark looks and muttered threats. But everyone knows her. Courtesy and modesty perished in the world of travel on the day when she took her first journey; but it will not be long before she is in hourly danger of extinction, for there are strong men in our midst.

There are other types of railway travellers, not so offensive as the above, which combines all the bad qualities, but still annoying in a varying degree to most of us; and of these others I will enumerate one or two of the commonest. First, there are those who, when they would go on a journey, take all their odd chattels and household utensils and parcel them up in brown paper, disdaining such things as boxes and trunks; furthermore, when such eccentrics have loaded themselves up with queer-shaped packages they will cast about for baskets of fruit and bunches of flowers to add to their own and other people's misery. Then there are the simple folks who are for ever eating and drinking in railway carriages. No sooner are they settled in their seats but they are passing each other tattered sandwiches and mournful scraps of pastry, and talking with their mouths full, and scattering crumbs over the trousers of fastidious old gentlemen. Sometimes they will peel and eat bananas with such rapidity that nervous onlookers are compelled to seek another compartment.

Some children do not make good travelling companions, for they will do nothing but whimper and howl throughout a journey, or they will spend all their time daubing their faces with chocolate or trying to climb out of the window. And the cranks are always with us; on the bleakest day, they it is who insist on all the windows being open, but in the sultriest season they go about in mortal fear of draughts, and will not allow a window to be touched.

More to my taste are the innocents who always find themselves in the wrong train. They have not the understanding necessary to fathom the timetables, nor will they ask the railway officials for advice, so they climb into the first train that comes, and trust to luck. When they are being hurtled towards Edinburgh, they will suddenly look round the carriage and ask, with a mild touch of pathos, if they are in the right train for Bristol. And then, puzzled and disillusioned, they have to be bundled out at the next station, and we see them no more. I have often wondered if these simple voyagers ever reach their destinations, for it is not outside probability that they may be shot from station to station, line to line, until there is nothing mortal left of them.

Above all other railway travellers, I envy the mighty sleepers, descendants of the Seven of Ephesus. How often, on a long, uninteresting journey, have I envied their sweet oblivion. With Lethe at their command, no dull, empty train journey, by day or night, has any terrors for them. Knowing the length of time they have to spend in the train, they compose themselves and are off to sleep in a moment, probably enjoying the gorgeous adventures of dream while the rest of us are looking blankly out of the window or counting our fingers. Two minutes from their destination they stir, rub their eyes, stretch themselves, collect their baggage, and, peering out of the window, murmur: 'My station, I think.' A moment later they go out, alert and refreshed, Lords of Travel, leaving us to our boredom.

Seafaring men make good companions on a railway journey. They are always ready for a pipe and a crack with any man, and there is usually some entertaining matter in their talk. But they are not often met with away from the coast towns. Nor do we often come across the confidential stranger in an English railway carriage, though his company is inevitable on the Continent, and, I believe, in America. When the confidential stranger does make an appearance here, he is usually a very dull dog, who compels us to yawn through the interminable story of his life, and rides some wretched old hobby-horse to death.

There is one more type of traveller that must be mentioned here, if only for the guidance of the young and simple. He is usually an elderly man, neatly dressed, but a little tobacco-stained, always seated in a corner, and he opens the conversation by pulling out a gold hunter and remarking that the train is at least three minutes behind time. Then, with the slightest encouragement, he will begin to talk, and his talk will be all of trains. As some men discuss their acquaintances, or others speak of violins or roses, so he talks of trains, their history, their quality, their destiny. All his days and nights seem to have been passed in railway carriages, all his reading seems to have been in timetables. He will tell you of the 12.35 from this place and the 3.49 from the other place, and how the 10.18 ran from So-and-so to So-and-so in such a time, and how the 8.26 was taken off and the 5.10 was put on; and the greatness of his subject moves him to eloquence, and there is passion and mastery in his voice, now wailing over a missed connection or a departed hero of trains, now exultantly proclaiming the glories of a non-stop express or a wonderful run to time. However dead you were to the passion, the splendour, the pathos, in this matter of trains, before he has done with you you will be ready to weep over the 7.37 and cry out in ecstasy at the sight of the 2.52.

Beware of the elderly man who sits in the corner of the carriage and says that the train is two minutes behind time, for he is the Ancient Mariner of railway travellers, and will hold you with his glittering eye.

25
Terminating

PAUL JENNINGS

This is the mystery of all railways, perhaps of all travel; the combination of the essential and serious, of journeys and freight routes that could be predicted by any economics or geography teacher, with the frivolous and unpredictable. One is always hearing how holidays and excursions are a modern luxury unknown to the great mass of Victorians. The early history of the Colne Valley Railway is one of local people, hoping for a branch line from the Eastern Union (who were themselves dwarfed by the powerful and greedy Eastern Counties) finally deciding, at a meeting in Halstead Town Hall in 1856, to go ahead and build their own line. The early directors, typical serious-looking gentlemen with beards or sideburns, look as if they were all perfectly capable of grinding the faces of the poor; and the capital which was somewhat painfully scraped together was certainly not intended to provide giddy excursions.

They opened the six-mile stretch from Chappel and Wakes Colne (junction with the existing line from Marks Tey to Sudbury) to Halstead in 1860. All that remains of Halstead Station now is the goods shed, of which the heavy padlocked doors are all covered with notices saying *E.M.D. KEEP OUT*. It is full of thousands of dusty cardboard containers for the electric motors made for lawn-mowers and washing machines by Electric and Mechanical Development, Ltd, who run the factory across the vacant space where the tracks and sidings were. But when the line was opened the vast weatherboarded Town Mill had already been housing the crêpe throwing and weaving machinery of the first Samuel Courtauld since 1825 (it still stands, and is still Courtaulds. The whole empire began from a mill at Pebmarsh, a few miles away). And when work began in 1860 on the extension to Haverhill the first sod was turned on June 19th by Miss Gurteen, of the Haverhill family whose cotton mills still employ many local people.

Serious industrial interests, not to mention the produce of a rich agricultural area. Yet the national pattern created by the unexpected zest for travelling of all classes (it was not until 1865 that national freight receipts exceeded those for pasenger traffic) was repeated here. How drab the opening of a new bypass or motorway is compared with all those gala nineteenth-century openings! Essex and Suffolk people are not noted for volatile, Provençal gaiety, but when the railway got as far as Castle Hedingham on July 31st, 1861, people 'were roused from the even tenor of their ways by a merry peal from the church tower, a fluttering of flags and the inspiring strains of the brass band of the 12th Essex Rifles', as related in the *Halstead Gazette*.

There were cheap fares for those celebrating the Hedingham opening (fourpence return to Halstead, sixpence to Chappel); and *seventeen hundred* people travelled, seven hundred of them from Halstead itself, where there was an arch of evergreens over the level crossing displaying the words *Progress and Prosperity*. Once Haverhill was reached there was a connection to Cambridge, and the first excursion there, on September 28th, 1865, was more or less a public holiday in Halstead; shops closed, houses near the station were decked with flags and streamers, and the Editor of the *Halstead Gazette* allowed it to come out a day earlier than usual so that the staff could go too.

This slightly festive note is a kind of counterpoint to the serious commercial history right up to our times. There soon began to be through excursions to Clacton, generally timed by the C.V.R. management near the full moon so that the country people could see to get home. At Birdbrook, on the Haverhill—Cambridge stretch, I spoke to a man who came out of the trim Victorian house, one of two set in the middle of fields, right by the broken bridge across a little curving road that ran up to a horizon of brilliant green young crops against the sky. He had lived there for fifty years, the cry of steam whistles across this secret valley on dark winter nights was part of his past, the little station drive now led up past his house merely to three new farm sheds where the station had been. 'Ah, we used to have fun watching the Sunday excursions,' he said. 'They used to stop here, with those old Colne Valley engines, then they couldn't start up the hill again, they'd take the people on, then go back to have a run at it. Poor tools altogether, they were.'

At Colne Engaine, across the road, from where the level crossing was, you can walk—indeed, you can drive—along a shallow cutting; only three years after the last train, but already there are saplings three or four feet high, willowherb, and marguerite daisies, the hollows between the sleeper beds are already levelling up—this regular indentation is not going to last as long as the rolling waves of the old ridged medieval fields in the Midlands. The cutting leads to a bridge, you can stand on the immense solid timbers looking down at weeds waving in the shallow Colne; a few more yards, and there is a wire fence, just before the brick abutment of a dismantled bridge over a meadow path. From the other abutment the line goes, under poplar trees, through someone else's land.

The continuity has gone. Standing in the fields, hearing nothing but birds, the wind in the trees, the occasional far-off lorry, even if you have walked less than half a mile along the track, you have a curious intimation of what it was the railways destroyed—the sheer brute mysterious fact of *distance*. Now that there are no thrumming telephone wires, no bright rails with metallic rumours of every bustling town in the country, you can sense what it was like here when the navvies came and laid these straight lines across the rambling parishes a century ago.

There is a mystery in all beginnings, and the most mysterious place on the line is a hundred yards or so up from Chappel and Wakes Colne station. You stand looking up the straight rails of a living line (now itself threatened); ahead to Sudbury and Bury St Edmunds, behind to Marks Tey, the junction on the main line from Liverpool Street to Colchester, Ipswich, Norwich, Yarmouth. And slightly to your left, there are, at most, fifty yards of trackless, sleeperless, overgrown line, ending at a fence beyond which is a bank of sloping land, recently mechanically graded and carrying a young orchard. Here, so close to the beginning, all trace of the line is destroyed, until you pick it up again on the other side of this estate.

Graham Finlayson* and I were there on a still, marvellously warm June afternoon, the kind of day that Constable painted, that one dreams about in the winter; a day when a gentle warm wind moved through the heavy summer trees, flowed visibly in silvered waves over the tall green crops, and swayed the yellow flowers growing profusely up through the deserted platforms. The station lane curved up under high hedges to its little cul-de-sac. Two cars were parked there, covered with leaves, as if belonging to travellers who had never been able to get back (in fact, they belonged to London commuters; *that* service has actually been improved since the C.V.R. closure). A square, box-like house still bore a sign over a side porch saying that the Railway Inn, C. Taberner, was licensed for the consumption of alcoholic liquor on the premises and similar wild debaucheries. It is now just Mr Taberner's house, but there was no sign of him or of anyone else. His garage door creaked in the wind. The hot sun shone on the elaborate Victorian foliate brickwork of the station building. There was no one there either, although a bottle of milk outside the station house door, its neat garden, and the mowed grass verge opposite, by the cornfield hedge, and the clothes-line stretched above it, showed that someone still lived here.

The door of the deserted signal box was open. Big clumsy old electrical equipment littered the floor, including the massive cast-iron device into which the signalman had to put the staff, received from the engine driver on this single-line working, before he could release the signal; and there were rows of primitive square glass cells containing dirty yellow liquid which stirred a schoolboy memory of elementary physics: *Leclanché cells*.

There were dusty notices, as though the men had gone away in the middle of everything, simply abandoning their 42 signals. *Name and addresses of Fogsignalmen*, said a dusty

* photographer. The best.

form on a spike; *arrangements for calling signalmen.* Written across under the last two columns were the words *None available.*

A Bardic Handlamp has been issued for use in your Signal Box. The lamp is stamped and serially numbered. Will you please therefore acknowledge this lamp on the enclosed sheet. Why *therefore*, one wondered? And what could a Bardic Handlamp *be*? It seemed appropriate now; one could imagine wild and plangent verses being intoned by its fitful beams, sad harp music coming from the shuttered waiting-room on rainy October nights. . . .

Haverhill station stands above the town, which also gives the casual passer-through a predominantly nineteenth-century impression. A pretty sleepy and unchanging place it must have been until recently—although Gurteens still employ a large number of people (a Miss Gurteen, it will be remembered, cut the first sod of the Halstead–Haverhill extension on June 19th, 1860). Over the green horizon on the far side of the station now creep enormous estates, for Haverhill and the G.L.C. are co-operating in a large overspill scheme that will raise the population from eleven to over eighteen thousand. New industries are moving in, from Pye electronics (based in nearby Cambridge) and oil-drilling equipment makers to I.F.F., which stands for International Flavours and Fragrances.

The empty station, next to a huge yard where vast lorries roar from a fuel depot with a 1,000-ton monthly turnover, stands between the old and the new. The station master's house, its windows boarded up, is at right angles to the platform, and from the platform wall one may look into the station master's garden. There is a big laburnum tree at the end. Although grass and weeds have run wild there are still straggly rose beds and vague asters and other domestic-looking flowers. It is very easy to imagine formal station master's teas, given every other Tuesday afternoon for the staff and friends, the station master's wife presiding, the young porters clumsy with the delicate cups and too bashful to ask for sugar, in a long sunlit Edwardian summer. There are thirty-seven minutes before the next train is due. Larks sing in the cloudless blue sky. Over the other wall of the garden a drayman is shouting at his heavy Suffolk Punches as they pull up the slope from the town. A bell rings somewhere down the platform. The station master consults his watch. 'Just go and relieve Mr Perkins in the Ticket Office, Joe.' The last two guests, a bank manager and his wife, are just taking their leave, a maid is clearing up (five cucumber sandwiches left) when the distant clanking of coupling rods announces the train . . .

The birds sang in the cloudless blue sky the day we were there. The buildings were covered with graffiti, most of them not reproducible. One, however, seemed significant— I am not sure of what. It said, in white chalk on green-painted wood:

BEECHING WAS FAB

(THE END.)

Acknowledgments

The editor and the publishers would like to express their gratitude to all who have granted permission for the inclusion of copyright material, or who have helped in the obtaining of that permission:

Penguin Books Ltd: for 'The Pioneers' from *Early British Railways* by Christian Barman, King Penguin Books, 1950, copyright © Christian Barman, pp. 12–16

Mr J. M. Fleming and Mr Angus MacLean: for 'Newcastle–Carlisle Opening' from *The Newcastle and Carlisle Railway* by the late John S. MacLean (R. Robinson & Co., 1948)

Mrs Sonia Rolt: for 'The Abbots Ripton Disaster' from *Red for Danger* by the late L.T.C. Rolt (Bodley Head, 1955)

Duckworth & Co. Ltd: for 'Saving a Train' from *Poetic Gems of William McGonagall* edited by James L. Smith

George Allen & Unwin: for 'Building the Bridge' from the *History of the Great Northern Railway* by C. H. Grinling

Granada Publishing Ltd: for 'Lust on the Line' from *The Beast in Man* by Emile Zola translated by Alec Brown

Chatto and Windus Ltd: for 'The Beauties' from *Select Tales of Anton Chekhov* translated by Constance Garnett

Penguin Books Ltd: for 'Last Journey' from *Anna Karenina* by Leo Tolstoy, Penguin Classics, revised ed. 1978, translated by Rosemary Edmonds, copyright © 1954, 1978 by Rosemary Edmonds, pp. 798–802

A. P. Watt Ltd, the National Trust and Macmillan London Ltd: for 'Uncovenanted Mercies', from *Limits and Renewals* by Rudyard Kipling